I0831805

The Dainty Decorator

By

Pauline Murfin

It would be difficult to say who got the biggest shock. While inspecting his newly renovated property in the village of Juniper, Architect Ben from Edinburgh, would come across what looked to him like a rather scruffy looking intruder sleeping in his bathtub.

Could things get any worse for village decorator Lizz? After being locked in her clients bathroom, than being picked up in the rain by him after her trusty little van ran out of petrol.

Ben hadn't realised how tired and overworked he had become until a brush with reality made him up sticks and move to the country. Little did he realise this dainty decorator fiddle player would open up his world to the pleasure of folk music and so much more.

Pauline Murfin is a sixty two year old mother, with three grown up sons. Married for forty three years to husband Graham, they live in a remote village in Northumberland. Pauline and her husband Graham moved to a small village which is part of the Kielder Forest in the Northumberland National Park in 1999. Poor health prevented Pauline from working, so she decided to study for a degree with The Open University. "To keep my brain ticking over", after completing her degree and gaining a Bachelor of Science she turns her hand to writing fiction. "Something I have always wanted to do" says Pauline.

Also by Pauline K Murfin

To Begin Again
Comraich
Dreams Lost Dreams Found
The Silent Connection

This book is dedicated to my friends and family. Without whose help it would not have been possible.

To my dear friends Blanche and Elizabeth, thank you once again. My two wonderful proof readers – who continue to enjoy a good laugh at the expense of my grammar and spelling errors.

To Blanche who can always find time for me, even with her very busy grandparent duties.

To Elizabeth, who continues to work tirelessly on improving my English.

To Pat Potts, an avid reader of Murfin books.

To Graham my technical support team, thank you.

To my copy editor, Lori Heaford. Thank you Lori, once again for your sympathetic interpretation of my manuscript.

And finally, thank you to Val McMahon, who inspired me to begin writing again.

Chapter 1

Liz Cassidy, alias 'The Dainty Decorator', as she was known locally, was putting the final touches to her latest job. This was to redecorate a beautiful old Victorian house for her newest client, an architect from Edinburgh. The house had been sympathetically renovated as per her client's instructions and she had been drafted in to do the final decoration.

This job had been a welcome change from the work she had become bogged down with lately. Liz felt a little guilty even thinking like that. However, she did sometimes feel like a resident in the sheltered housing developments where most of her business came from.

This job had been inspiring. She had been given more or less a free hand and a rough colour scheme to work with. The solicitor who had handled the sale of the property had once been a client of hers. And he had recommended her to the new owner of the beautiful house on the edge of the village.

The house was a builder's and decorator's dream – beautiful old character features, large fireplaces in every room, fabulous deep architraves and cornices, with wonderfully carved archways in the large tiled entrance hall. It had large bay windows, with full instructions that they must be restored and not simply replaced with plastic.

Liz was bone tired, and all she had left to do was to put the door handle and finger plates back on to the large bathroom door then she could pack up and go. A distant holler from the last of the builders came from downstairs, reminding her to shut the windows before leaving. All the windows were open in order to hasten the drying of the paint before the client arrived at the weekend.

As the front door slammed so did the bathroom door, where Liz was just about to fit the door handle.

Uh-oh, thought Liz with the door handle still in her hand and unattached from the door, which was now firmly stuck to the newly painted frame.

“Oh no, please, God, no. This can’t be happening,” Liz said to herself, trying not to become overly worried, despite the tide of panic that was beginning to rise up into her throat. She shouted rather excitedly, and rather louder than she had intended.

“Hello! Hello! Is anyone still downstairs? Bob? Harry? Tony? Anyone? Oh nooooo!”

The enormity of her situation was beginning to filter through to Liz’s vivid imagination. First she thought about the house being on the edge of the village, off the beaten track, so shouting out of the window was a bit of a waste of time. Her phone, she realised, was in her van, which was parked outside on the drive.

She hadn’t bothered bringing her tool bag in as she had completed the main work yesterday and had only come back to do the finishing touches, such as fitting the door knobs and the finger plates and retrieving her dust sheets. How simple should that have been, Liz thought to herself, so how on earth was she in this situation?

Liz looked around the newly decorated bathroom to see if there was anything that could be used to lever the door open. At first she shied away from prising or prodding anything into her meticulously painted door and frame. Then, as common sense suggested to her that she could be here until tomorrow at some distant time in the day, she reminded herself that the door could always be repainted.

Yet, she had cleaned everything but the dust sheets up in the morning, and all she had in her dungarees pocket now was a tape measure, a small screwdriver, some screws and a handful of rawl plugs. After much deliberating about the damage a screwdriver would make in an attempt to lever the door open, she decided that, on the whole, she hadn't any choice.

"Well, here goes. God, it pains me to do this after finishing the door so perfectly, not to mention the bloody frame. But it's only work; it can be redone," Liz said to no one in particular and began to push the screwdriver into the door frame – gently to begin with, then more forcefully as it soon became obvious that she could hack at it all day and it wasn't going to shift this heavy Victorian door from the frame.

Realisation began to set in. Liz remembered that she had been told that the client was coming down at the weekend, to see all the work and arrange his move if everything was completed. Tonight was Friday. Her tummy was rumbling as she had intended to buy a takeaway on the way home.

Oh, thought Liz, there goes my hot bath for my weary limbs, and my takeaway in front of a cosy fire. Well, at least the van is safe enough on the drive.

There would be a puddle when she got home, left by Barnie, her Irish wolfhound, who wouldn't be best pleased at not having his walk and sniff round the common. She looked around for somewhere to sleep. Well, in a bathroom the only obvious place was the bath. And the only thing available to cover herself with was her one remaining dust sheet that she hadn't already packed in the van.

To lighten the moment Liz comforted herself with thinking that at least it wasn't an empty bedroom. At least in here she had a loo. She was so tired and, with nothing better to do but worry, she climbed into the bath and covered herself with the large dust sheet. It did cross her mind, whimsically, that she could actually take a bath, it being a bathroom, after all. Then she remembered that the very, very expensive, posh boiler had not yet been lit.

Her client, the architect, who was from Edinburgh, Liz reminded herself, was a bit of a green conservationist and had kept all the original features of the property, which Liz approved of. He'd had the most beautiful red Rayburn fitted in the kitchen, which Liz absolutely loved, and which would be run from the most futuristic boiler system. Apparently it was what they called a biomass boiler, which would save fifty to sixty per cent of the fuel costs, or so she had been told by the fitter of said heating system, while she was decorating the kitchen. He had explained to Liz, quite seriously, how, with the solar panels and the pellet and log burning system in use, it would heat this whole house while conserving energy.

Liz thought she would always remember what a biomass boiler was now that it had been explained in such detail. Anyway, thought Liz, I digress. All of that heating system and still no hot water for a longed for bath.

After half an hour's worrying about all the things she could do nothing about while stuck in a bathtub, tiredness began to have more of an effect, overriding her panic. As Liz was so tired she could have slept on the proverbial clothes line, she drifted off to sleep.

Chapter 2

It would seem to anyone normal that to fall asleep, locked in a bathroom, all alone in an empty house would be impossible. However, Liz was so tired and had so many commitments, being the most recommended decorator in the village – well, actually the only decorator in the village – that she could have worked night and day and still never satisfied everyone.

If Nigel had his way she wouldn't ever stop to eat or sleep, except with him, but that was another story. Nigel was Liz's man friend. You couldn't possibly say boyfriend when referring to Nigel as Liz was sure he had never been a boy. He'd come fully grown or so it would seem.

Even Nigel's job was, well, how could you put it? Stuffy. He taught maths in the local high school. God help those who had to listen to him all day. Nigel was an organiser – of other people's lives, especially Liz's.

He was always involved in some good cause or other. However, he simply walked about with his very important clipboard in his hand while he delegated all the actual work to unsuspecting newcomers to the village or to Liz.

As well as decorating this beautiful old house for the last six weeks, Liz had been painting the scenery for the village hall Christmas panto, as well as trawling around the local charity shops in order to find suitable material with which to make costumes. Not to mention attempting to run her own home and walk her poor neglected dog. Even then she preferred to do all the things Nigel asked of her, as to complain would only bring on his 'busy man syndrome' where he walked around as though with a crown of thorns on his head.

So, in a nutshell, that was how Liz could fall asleep on a log if she happened to sit on one. She must have been deep in her slumber and didn't hear the first one or two gentle but forceful pushes on the bathroom door. At the same instant that a full-grown man burst into the room, Liz shot up from her dust sheet gasping and yelping.

It was difficult to say who had got the biggest fright, the man who had been flung into the bathroom by the force of his push on the door, or Liz who had shot bolt upright from her deep and much-needed slumber. Whatever, they were both equally shocked to find another person in the otherwise empty house at midnight.

At first Ben guessed it to be a child asleep in the bath, a squatter maybe? She was certainly a dirty little thing, he thought. What a cheek.

"What the hell?"

Ben couldn't believe it. He hadn't even moved away from the city yet, in to his country idyll, and he had a squatter.

"Who, may I ask, are you? And what are you doing in my house?"

Ben found the cord for the light and the uncovered bulb glared down on to Liz, who was still sitting bolt upright in the bath, feeling as though she were being grilled while suffering from sleep deprivation. She managed to stutter her name.

"I'm Liz, the decorator. Erm… I got stuck in the bathroom when the door slammed shut."

She felt such a fool, until her senses began to arrive, a bit late, she thought, making her look like a gibbering gnome, as sitting down she was even smaller than her full height of four feet ten inches.

Squinting up into the bright light, she looked at what appeared to be a giant's dark, chiselled features, with Hugh Grant type black hair flopping forward as he leaned over the bath to take in the sight of his intruder. Liz tried her best to look indignant but failed miserably, owing to the fact that she was still sitting down and did indeed look like a child in the bath.

Right, that's enough, she thought, pulling herself together and out of her exhausted stupor. She stood up. With the benefit of the feet on the bath she appeared a little taller, giving her more courage to look into the face of her addresser.

"My name is Liz Cassidy. I am the decorator of this property; and who, may I ask, are you?"

Liz had guessed who it was but she just wanted to get her own back and put him on the back foot. It also gave her a chance to pull herself together and climb out of the bath, in order to feel less conspicuous.

"I am Ben Paris, the owner of this house," said Ben, while smiling to himself at the ridiculousness of the situation, but none the less enjoying the spark of indignation being emitted from this tiny ball of fire. She indeed looked no more than a child. Surely, he thought, this must be the decorator's apprentice? It couldn't actually be the decorator, could it?

Liz gathered up the dust sheet as best she could and visibly stood taller in an effort to give her the confidence to walk to the door without feeling a fool for locking herself in the bathroom in the first place. She mumbled something about sending him her invoice at a later date and walked stiffly out and down the stairs.

Ben almost burst out laughing when the tiny figure left through the front door, slamming it behind her.

"Well, it could only happen in the country," he said to no one in particular; and, after a glance at the retreating little van, went to inspect his new home.

Liz had dumped the dust sheet in the van and prayed the van would start so that she could escape any prying eyes from the house, before she collapsed into a heap with the embarrassment of it all.

As Liz drove down the gravel drive, getting to the gates at the end of the drive, she could see that the petrol light was glowing on the dashboard and had started to ping now to tell her she was dangerously low on petrol.

“Oh bugger, that’s all I bloody need.” Liz could hear Nigel’s voice in her head saying there was no need to swear and he wished she wouldn’t. But she could also hear her best friend Isabel’s voice saying, “Sod off, Nigel.”

Liz afforded herself a grin. That was what she needed – a few deep breaths and a good laugh about the whole situation and she would feel a whole lot better about looking a total fool in front of her gorgeous and previously unseen client.

Liz was just beginning to feel in control of the situation, so she made her mind up to nip to the Tesco all-night garage, fill up, and get herself a takeaway and a nice bottle of wine at the same time. Liz heaved a sigh of relief and was about to smile about the whole sorry episode when the little van started to spit and chug. She tried to give it a bit more throttle but it made no effort to keep going and shuddered to a stop, the petrol light giving her the evil eye and pinging and dinging just to make things worse.

"Oh shut up, you bloody stupid thing. I know, I can hear you, I'm not deaf."

Liz turned the engine off and laid her head on the steering wheel, telling herself that this could not be happening.

"I don't believe this. Can anything else happen? Is there anything else up there ready to drop its lot on my tired little head?"

After Liz had ranted and raved, venting her spleen, she decided it was no good. She had to sort herself out and stop feeling sorry for herself. She collected her purse and petrol can out of the back of the van, and pulled on her old duffle coat. It was filthy and covered in paint, but it was, after all, for work, and wasn't meant to be a fashion statement. She locked the van, which was ironic as no one could pinch it anyway, and she started walking in the total darkness along the lonely country lane.

“This is great fun after a long day’s work, walking to Tesco’s in the pitch dark. All it needs now is to rain and my night will be complete.”

This was said into the night, where Liz didn’t actually care if anyone heard or not. After what seemed like a hundred miles of walking but was actually only about three, Liz could see the lights of the garage all bright and welcoming and she almost cheered. She arrived at the pump, filled her little can, and went inside to pay, knowing she had to walk back yet. But after collecting her wine and takeaway from the shop, she was sure she would feel a lot better.

When the young man behind the counter, which looked more like a glass cell, attempted to use the card that Liz had produced, there was an ominous silence. He tried it again and then delivered the earth-shattering news that the card was void.

“What do you mean it’s void? It can’t be.”

“I’m sorry,” said the spotty youth behind the glass. Now Liz knew why the glass was there – to protect him from irate customers, in the dead of night.

“It can’t be void, check the dates. It’s a fairly new card. I can show you other ID; hang on, I’ll show you my licence.”

Liz scrabbled about, getting her licence out of her purse, only to be told by the spotty youth, who was looking decidedly embarrassed, that there was nothing she could produce that would allow her to buy anything using that card. In fact, by law, he had to keep the card until it was investigated.

Now Liz definitely knew that the skinny, spotty youth was entombed in the glass case in order to stop the general public from killing him in a fit of temper. Liz turned stiffly, looking longingly at the can of petrol on the floor, and part of her wanted to pick it up and run with it. She wondered how long it would take him to get out of his protective bubble and chase her in order to retrieve it. On a good day she thought she could possibly outrun him, but she was so exhausted that he could have rugby tackled her within yards, so that was not a good idea.

She plodded out of the petrol station and away from the lovely welcoming lights of the supermarket, back towards her abandoned van in the pitch dark, where, Liz thought helplessly, her phone was.

Oh why, oh why, had she not brought her phone with her out of the van? she thought. At least she could have rung Isabel for help. Well, one thing Liz knew for sure was that there was definitely some rotten little bad luck goblin out to get her tonight. When she eventually got home to her lovely warm bed, she intended to stay there until at least ten in the morning. No matter where she was supposed to be she was going to treat herself to a long lie-in.

There was only tonight to sort out first. She started back towards her van, trying her best to be positive, striding out as purposefully as she could… Suddenly she felt huge blobs of rain, lightly at first. Then they began to get faster and heavier until Liz turned her face skywards to shout out loud, “You rotten bastard!”

It had all become just a little too much for Liz, and she added her own fat tears of self-pity to the already huge blobs of rain falling from the sky. As she plodded along in the darkness, where no street lights existed, Liz’s heart was down in the deepest part of her boots. Just then the lights from a car in the distance made her move to one side. That was all she needed, Liz thought to herself, to get knocked down in the dark and no one knowing who she was. Liz knew just how George Bailey had felt when no one had recognised him in *It’s A Wonderful Life*. All she wanted now was an angel called Clarence to come along and help her home.

As Liz dwelt on thoughts of Clarence coming to help, the passing car slowed up beside her. A kerb crawler would just about finish her night off nicely, she told herself.

Liz heard the hum of the electric window and a vaguely familiar voice shouted, “Do your parents know you are out? Are you all right? Can I help you at all?”

When Liz turned her face towards the voice, which she had heard only hours before, her face partially obscured by her hood, she had to make an instant decision. Did she want to look a fool twice in one night with the same man? Or did she want to get home and go to bed and forget that this night had ever happened? No decision. She was tired, cold and wet; she would swallow her pride and ask for help.

Liz pulled her hood back and peered into the warm and welcoming interior of the very swish car, letting its occupant see who the stranger in the darkness was.

Chapter 3

"Hello again. I'm sure there is a perfectly good reason why you are walking along an unlit country road, in the middle of the night, not to mention the fact that you are probably soaked through."

This was said with a derisory up and down look at her duffle coat. This cannot be happening to me. I simply cannot believe it's happening to me, Liz thought. Now he is worried about me dripping all over his cream leather interior. Oh God, how embarrassing. Can it get any worse than this?

As the dark, chiselled face leaned over towards the passenger side Liz could see his expression and she could have sworn that he was smirking. It could just have been her imagination, she admitted.

"Get in out of the rain, for goodness sake, you must be freezing. You left the house ages ago – where on earth have you been until this hour?"

Liz climbed in through the passenger side door, trying her best to levitate above the seat in order not to damage his lovely clean cream leather. However, as that was impossible she simply sat in one little heap and didn't move. She was worried, as he had the heater on full blast, that if she didn't get out soon she would start to steam. Wouldn't that be a nice smell? Wet wool!

"Which way?"

"Sorry?"

"Which way are we going in order to get you back home?"

Feeling very flustered, wet and sorry for herself, not to mention mortally embarrassed, Liz gave her knight in shining armour, or was it her 'Clarence', directions to her cottage. Trust her to get an angel that made her feel like a child and a fool all in one night.

"Wasn't that your van I saw a couple of miles back? I wondered why it was parked in the middle of nowhere."

Deciding she had to come clean, as there was no other way of explaining – and didn't everyone, at some point, run out of petrol at least once in their lifetime? – she confessed.

"I ran out of petrol," Liz mumbled into her duffle coat.

An "Oh," said with a slight cough, told Liz that he found it amusing, but was attempting not to capitalise on her distress. I suppose that's something, thought Liz.

"I was trying to finish the painting this afternoon as I had been told that the owner of the house – erm, you, presumably – was coming down at the weekend. And all I had left to do was put the bathroom door handle and the finger plates on and I was finished. I had all the windows open to get rid of the smell of the paint and, unfortunately, when one of the builders slammed the front door… Voilà! It also slammed the bathroom door. My intention was to go to the garage when I finished work, but the rest, as they say, is history."

"But weren't you coming from the other direction?"

Oh God, thought Liz, he wasn't going to be satisfied until he had got every gory detail and she may as well just get it said and then she could forget it forever.

"I took my can and walked to the garage, which, I might say, is quite a hike when you've been at work since seven the previous morning. I filled up my can and thought my troubles were almost over, only to be told that my card has been compromised and the spotty little devil wouldn't give me the petrol. Hence my walk back empty-handed."

"Oh, you poor thing. It really hasn't been your night, and to top the lot I noticed it started to rain just as I left the house. Listen, why don't I double back to the garage and collect your petrol can? Then at least you can get your van started, which will save you a lot of trouble in the morning."

"No, no, don't bother, please. I'll be happy just to get home and go to bed. I will ask my friend to take me to the garage in the morning, after I've sorted this bother with my card being compromised."

Their journey had brought them back on to the lighted roads so her driver afforded himself a glance over to his passenger, who had relaxed slightly after divulging her night's catastrophes. He could see that she was not as young as he had first though. In fact she looked to be in her late twenties or early thirties. She had an elfin-shaped face, he thought, and her eyes, which he caught a quick glimpse of, seemed huge, although she looked very tired. She had short-cropped, dark hair – and that was about all he could take in while driving.

Following her instructions through the village past Ben's own driveway, he arrived at a thatched cottage with an archway of dormant roses over the tiny gate. Liz didn't think she could have been happier to see her little cottage again. She imagined her comfy warm bed, then, more urgently, poor Barnie, who must have thought he had been abandoned by now.

"I can't thank you enough, Mr err…"

"Paris, Ben Paris."

"Mr Paris."

"Ben, please. Just call me Ben."

"Thank you again, Ben, I can't tell you how grateful I am. If I thought I could stay awake long enough I would ask you in for a coffee, but I think I would fall asleep before the kettle boiled, I'm afraid. I'm sorry. I hope I haven't taken you too far out of your way? I never even asked where you are staying this evening."

"Well, actually, I'm driving back to Edinburgh. I wasn't supposed to come down until tomorrow with the removal van, when the house was completely finished, but I couldn't wait. I had nothing better to do so I nipped down. However, like you, I hadn't realised how tiring it would be driving both ways in one night after working all day."

"Oh." Oh, indeed, thought Liz. He was going to drive all the way back to Edinburgh tonight? But it's almost three o'clock in the morning! she thought in surprise after looking at her watch in the dim light – God, no wonder she was tired. Then she knew what she was going to say even before it had popped out of her mouth. Well, she reasoned with herself, if he had wanted to murder her he could have done it on the unlit country road. He wouldn't have waited until they were safely back at her own cottage. Oh God, here goes, Liz thought. Heaven knows what Nigel will say about this!

"Look, you can't travel all the way back to Edinburgh tonight. You are welcome to sleep in my son's bed. After all, you did rescue me tonight."

"Oh, I couldn't impose upon you. Besides, if I was to sleep in your son's bed where would he sleep?"

"Oh, he is at university in Edinburgh."

"You have a son at university?" This was said with incredulity in his voice, as though she couldn't possibly be old enough to have a grown-up son.

"Ha, yes, I'm older than I look. But listen, God knows what I am about to face. I left my dog at seven this morning and he hasn't been out all day for a…well, to relieve himself, so I'm sorry in advance for what we may find. I hope you have a strong stomach."

"Well, if you are absolutely sure about me staying? I promise you faithfully that I am an architect and of honest and sober disposition. I also promise not to murder you in your bed. In fact, I'll be perfectly happy to sleep in a chair downstairs."

Chapter 4

Thank goodness, thought Liz, her first piece of good luck tonight. Somehow, and she would never know how, Barnie, poor dog, had held not only his water but everything else too until he heard her key in the door. The first thing Liz did was to hurry to the back door to open it for Barnie to dash out into the little garden. She never, ever normally let him into the garden, as being a wolfhound he needed lots of long runs and plenty of exercise, but just this once needs must.

The poor dog seemed to be outside for ages. Liz could only imagine the relief he must have felt. When he eventually padded back inside he came face to face with a stranger. Ben, who had followed Liz through to the kitchen, was taken back at the size of Barnie. He had never actually seen an Irish wolfhound close up and was quite shocked at how tall they were.

Barnie was the most unaggressive dog, and pushed his face into Ben's hand for him to stroke him and say hello, which Ben did, as he loved dogs.

"Hello, and who are you, big fella?"

"This is Barnie. He is a great big softy and I can only say that he has performed a miracle today by not leaving a huge puddle on the floor. For that I am eternally grateful," Liz said while stroking Barnie's head vigorously, telling him he was a good old dog. She automatically put some food in his bowl and water in his dish. She then opened the lid on her Aga and put the kettle on to boil. Even though she was bone tired she would have to have something to eat and drink as she hadn't eaten since before lunchtime and she presumed Mr err, Ben, hadn't either.

She quickly closed the curtains, switched the lamps on and laid the table in the kitchen, which was where she tended to live most of the time. Somehow, tired though she was, Liz managed to make hot drinks and omelettes for two. It was reasonably sensible food for the middle of the night, she considered. She pointed her late visitor in the direction of Tom's bedroom then flopped into her cosy bed, stopping only to put warm pyjamas on.

Chapter 5

Liz was warm and comfortable and felt as though she had slept the clock round as she gradually opened her eyes and became conscious. It began to dawn on her that it was lighter than it normally was when she woke up. A quick look at her watch made her gasp in horror, to realise that it was eleven thirty. Then she gasped a second time as she suddenly remembered Mr err, her visitor.

"Oh my God," she said aloud and leapt out of bed.

After she had scrambled around to find her dressing gown and slippers she hurried across to peep into Tom's room to see if her visitor was also still asleep. However, Tom's bed was made and, as a quick look in through the open bathroom door revealed no one, she hurried downstairs to find no one there either.

Liz was beginning to wonder if last night had been an apparition when her eyes suddenly noticed a piece of paper folded against a marmalade pot on the kitchen table. She hurriedly opened the note, which read:

Thank you very much for your kindness in allowing me to sleep in your son's bed. I hope by now you trust that I was not a mad murderer who picked you up in the night. I took Barnie out for a short walk. I would have liked to have taken him for longer but maybe I can do that another day. Your van is outside, a small thank you for my bed and board. Must go now to meet the removal van. I'm sure I will be seeing you very soon.

Ben

Liz read and re-read the short note. It seemed impossible, the whole night from the moment she had been locked inside the bathroom to now. She was sat at the kitchen table with a mug of steaming coffee, trying to make sense of the last twenty-four hours, when her phone rang. She moved with her mug in her hand to answer the phone and heard Tom's frantic voice, which sounded just like his father's when he was worried.

"Oh my God, I was just about to get on a train and come home to see where you had got to. I rang your mobile at least ten times yesterday and left a message each time, then I rang home at least three times last night. I have been worried sick about you, where were you?"

"Sorry, Tom. It's a long story and I can hardly believe it myself, and I haven't had time to check any messages on either phone. You would not believe in a million years what happened to me yesterday. I am still having difficulty believing it myself."

Liz proceeded to tell Tom about the door and the petrol and her bank card. It wasn't until she got to the part about her visitor staying overnight that she wondered if it was wise to tell him. She chose not to mention it unless pressed. She did tell him she had only just jumped out of bed so she had better get a wriggle on and have a shower before either Nigel or Isabel arrived unexpectedly.

“Tell Nigel to bog off and have a day to yourself, Mum. You work too hard. You know you don’t have to do so much, we’re not on the breadline. It makes me feel very guilty, you toiling away while I live the life of a very, very hard-working student.”

This was said tongue in cheek and with his re-emerging good humour. Liz was relieved that he sounded more cheerful and less stressed. He worried. Since Robert had died, he’d taken his role as the man of the house quite seriously. Even though he was a student, he was a very sensible young man. Quite often it was Liz who encouraged Tom to go to parties or have a drink and enjoy his time at university. After all, to become a doctor was a long hard road, so he may as well enjoy life at the same time, she would tell him.

“I will tell Nigel, I will, honestly. I’ll tell him you’ll punch him in the nose if he doesn’t give me a rest.”

“Ha, you’re only kidding, but I would, given half the chance. Okay, I’ll catch ya later. Chill out for the rest of the day, promise?”

“I will, I will. Bye, love.”

Chapter 6

Feeling refreshed and contented, a feeling that she had almost forgotten existed, Liz decided on a quick shower, and then she donned her Saturday jeans, oversize sweater and wellington boots, which Barnie knew was a sign he was going to the common to stretch his long legs.

Liz was at her happiest while walking the dog on the local common, which was invariably devoid of other inhabitants. This gave her a chance to reason things out, reassure herself about a particular problem. Or simply relax, which was something she rarely gave herself time to do, because she knew that if she relaxed her thoughts would drift back to her earlier life with Bob.

Bob had not only been her husband but also her best friend; they had had so much in common. They'd both loved music and a good part of their lives had been spent playing in the group together. As Liz wandered aimlessly on the common, Barnie stretched his long, wiry limbs, running after every leaf that floated past. Liz's thoughts harked back to the day when she and Bob and the rest of the guys had decided on a name for their ensemble.

All kinds of ridiculous names had been thrown into the mix until someone had come up with the simplest suggestion. "We always finish on 'The Wild Rover', so why not simply The Rovers?" And that was that.

Liz played the fiddle, which her mother at first had taken umbrage at, after paying all those years for violin lessons, demanding, "And what do you do with it?" However, she'd soon come around – at least her lessons hadn't been entirely wasted.

Up until they had decided on their name they had simply been a group of musicians who happened to meet in the local pub and jam. The landlord of the Dog and Duck had realised very quickly that his takings were always up on a night when the group had played. He'd very quickly suggested putting posters up, advertising when there would be live music on, which was usually about twice a week.

Bob had played the banjo with such enthusiasm that it was impossible to keep your feet still. Tom had played the tin whistle from an early age, when most boys thought the recorder or anything similar was a girl's instrument. Tom had thought it was great that his parents were musicians and that it wasn't a sissy thing to do if your parents were 'in the business'. Mostly they had played The Dubliners' type of music, Irish and Scottish folk songs.

Angus, a huge bear of a man, played the Irish flute. The soft haunting sounds that emanated from it gave you shivers down your spine. Tony was their string man. He could more or less play anything with strings; but he kept to mostly the guitar and the mandolin, depending on the song. Ted was their accordion guy; and any one of them would play the bodhrán, the Irish drum, if a song required it.

Liz was miles away as she remembered how Angus would lift her up on a box or a speaker while she played the fiddle so that she could be seen. The audience thought it was a hoot as she was so small compared to him and, while playing, could do nothing about it.

Liz was so deep in thought that she nearly jumped out of her skin when someone tapped her on the shoulder.

"And where were you?"

"Christ, what a fright you gave me! I was miles away. I was working, erm, late, very late. You mean last night?"

"Yes… You sound guilty; now what have you been up to?"

"Nothing, you fool, you startled me, that's all."

"Yes, but when I asked where were you, you looked decidedly sheepish… Come on, spill the beans… Where and what have you been up to?"

Isabel Rowe, Liz's best friend from her school days, knew everything there was to know about Liz. She could sense when she was lying or even obfuscating, as she had once accused her of doing, at which Liz had giggled and said she wouldn't know about that as she hadn't a clue what it meant. Isabel had told her she knew very well what she meant by it, and she was still doing it – avoiding questions to avoid telling the truth.

Today, Isabel looked her usual fabulous self. Even when she was wearing her walking on the common clothes, she still managed to look as though she were at a fashion shoot. Married more times than she cared to remember, well, three times, she had decided this time she was staying 'strictly single from now on'.

She had made a packet out of each of her ex-husbands, so she had no need to find another man except for recreational purposes. She liked to have fun, she loved to go on dates, and she was very glam and had a figure that she knew exactly how to show off to its best advantage. If a man was single he was fair game. If he was married he was a no-no. One thing Isabel hated more than anything was a woman who stole other people's husbands, and she should know – she had lost two in just that way. Her first marriage, she would admit to anyone, had simply been a childhood fling on both sides and then they had grown up.

She couldn't stand Nigel, Liz's clingy man friend, and certainly didn't want to see her best friend lumbered with such a miserable pleb. Isabel could see quite plainly, and was forever telling Liz, that he was only interested in her because he wanted to move into her cottage. It would suit him down to the ground if Liz did all the DIY, the painting and the gardening, and he would take over the finances. Yes, she was sure he would, but Isabel was not going to let her best friend be hoodwinked by a boring toad like Nigel. Isabel quite often told Liz she would rather paint herself purple and shave all her hair off than let her marry him. Isabel wasn't the only one who felt that way about Niiigel. [Nigel had to be said in a whining voice because that was the way he was.] The group were also very protective of Liz since Bob's death. Nigel would have to get past each of them to reach Liz.

Isabel snuggled into her tan-coloured, deep pile sheepskin coat, worn with a cream roll-neck sweater, her long legs encased in chocolate brown cords and knee-length leather riding style boots. Beside her, Liz felt like her usual, gauche, ungainly, childish self, which was the way Isabel always made her feel. And yet she was perfectly dressed for walking a dirty great Irish wolfhound on the common on a damp autumn afternoon. If anything, it should have been Isabel that felt out of place; but Isabel could carry off an arctic fur coat in the middle of a heatwave and still look classy.

"How did you find me, anyway? I sneaked away so that Barnie and I could spend some quality time together. Poor dog nearly burst yesterday after being left until midnight…err, until I finished work. So I thought he deserved a treat."

"Ah-ha! I knew it! Mrs Mangle told me she'd seen a strange man driving your van early this morning just as she'd happened to open her curtains. And she said she'd seen you go out with Barnie in your wellies, so she knew you would be going to the common."

Mrs Mangle was Liz's nosey neighbour. She lived opposite Liz, and, even though Liz had a high privet hedge and roses around the arch over her gate, always managed to keep tabs on her every move.

"Oh all right, nosey knickers, it's getting so a girl can't sneeze before Mrs Mangle puts it in the local rag. Well, if you must know…"

"The truth now… I can see your little mind ticking over; you're going to try to give me the watered down version, and I warn you I will not stop probing until I get the whole truth."

This was said in Isabel's best interrogating manner, and Liz knew it was true; she wouldn't stop until she had all the gory details. Liz began to tell how she had almost finished the work on the old house – the house that Isabel had seen only from the outside, and could have fallen for herself. However, Isabel preferred to be amongst all the gossip, in the centre of the village, rather than on the outskirts.

Liz continued her story, wincing as she told Isabel how Ben, the new owner, had found her sitting in the bath covered in a dust sheet. And how she'd had to attempt a dignified exit, only to run out of petrol. Liz could see that Isabel was bursting with questions and almost splitting her sides laughing as she continued to regale her sorry tale. Becoming angry all over again with the spotty youth who had refused to give her any assistance when her card had quite obviously been compromised by a villain, Liz spluttered, "I mean, where the hell has chivalry gone, I ask you?" Liz still sounded irate even after a good night's sleep.

The next part was a bit tricky and Liz's narrative became a little hesitant, until Isabel reminded her, "The lot. Spill it – the whole truth and nothing but the truth."

"Well… Of course, after I had to leave the petrol station empty-handed and walk back in the rain, who should pull up beside me? God, I thought at first I was being propositioned until I recognised his voice. If there had been a big hole there, though, I would have jumped right in, no kidding."

Isabel was beside herself with curiosity and undisguised mirth at Liz's expense.

"Well, well, come on, out with it."

"All right. He gave me a lift back – it was either that or walk back in the middle of the night in the pouring rain. It turned out that he was going to drive all the way back to Edinburgh after dropping me off. But by then it was the middle of the night, and he was planning on coming back today. I reasoned that if he had been going to murder me he would have done it in the country lane, where no one would have been any the wiser. So I…let him sleep in Tom's room. There, are you satisfied?"

Liz blurted out, "He slept overnight in your house? Wow! No, of course I'm not satisfied. Good God, girl, I need details, innuendoes, impressions of the great man himself."

"I have no idea as I was so tired I could have slept on a clothes line. I told you, I'd been working non-stop, as we were told the owner had decided he wanted to move in today. All of us common workers had to be out by Friday at the latest. Honestly, all I had to do was fit the bloody door knob and then wham… It was all down hill from then on."

"Never mind that, what was he like? Was he good-looking? I already know he isn't married; I've heard that through the grapevine. I know he is an architect and has a practice in Edinburgh. Why is he moving to Juniper Green, of all places? Not that it isn't a lovely village, but is it going to be his holiday home or is he moving here full-time?"

"My God, you don't want to know much, do you? For goodness sake, let the man move in first before you start interrogating him."

"You must have seen if he was good-looking or not, surely?"

"Well, yes, I would say he is good-looking in a Hugh Grant sort of way. He's tall."

"Well, everyone is tall compared to you. That's saying nothing."

"Well, probably six foot, I think…erm nice-looking, nicely dressed, I think. Now, can we drop the subject?"

"Nearly. Why was he driving your van this morning?"

"Well, to be honest, I'm not sure myself. I was so tired I must have slept like a log and when I got up I realised he wasn't anywhere to be seen. I found a note on the kitchen table telling me he had taken Barnie for a walk and that my van was back as a sort of thank you for my hospitality. And that only means a bed for the night, before you read anything into it. So your guess is as good as mine. He said that he had to go to meet his removal van. So presumably he is at this precise moment moving into his newly painted house. Is that it? Can we forget it now?"

"Oh, you are hopeless. How on earth are we ever going to find out all the details if you, who had the golden opportunity to ask, didn't?"

"Isabel, much as this might shock you, I never thought. And I was so tired. And even if I did, I wouldn't have the cheek that you have. We will find out soon enough."

"Oohwa, I've just had a thought… Wait until Niiigel finds out that you had a man under your roof last night. Hee hee, what would your boyfriend think of that?"

“Nigel is not my boyfriend! At my age, one doesn’t have boyfriends; one has acquaintances,” Liz said in her best posh accent. “And, to be honest, I have no intentions of telling him or Tom, for that matter, so I would appreciate it if you would keep it shut. And no, I have nothing to hide, before you ask. But we both know that my life will not be worth living if either finds out that I let a man who picked me up in the middle of the night sleep under my roof.

“Actually, the reason I’ve left my phone at home while I’m out is because I know he will have rung at least three times. I’m supposed to be meeting him down at the village hall to paint the scenery for the Christmas panto. I haven’t checked my mobile since yesterday. In fact it’s still in the van. I know Tom was frantically looking for me but I have spoken to him and explained. But Nigel will be beside himself – you know what he’s like when he organises work parties and people don’t turn up.”

"Ah, I was hoping we could have gone into town shopping? Don't go. He will be just as angry with you being late as he will be if you don't turn up at all. Go on, go on."

"No, no, I can't. I'd love to but he will be like a bear with a sore head if I don't turn up – you know what he's like. Besides, the sooner I finish it, the sooner I will have my weekends back again. Then we can go, next weekend for sure. I promise, it's a date. Saturday, we'll shop till we drop, okay?"

"Well, all right. You're mad, though. If you think he won't have found another job for you by then you are sadly mistaken. But I'm holding you to it, so Saturday is a date and don't you dare break it."

Isabel gave Liz a hug and walked back to where she had parked her car. Liz threw the ball one last time for Barnie then told him it was time to go and face the music with Nigel.

Chapter 7

The village hall was a grand name for what was no more than a hut. However, the dilapidated place was in constant use for such things as Women's Institute meetings and all their jumble sales and tombolas, the village leek show, the Christmas pantomime, and even the keep fit and youth clubs, which was taking a bit of a risk as the floor was on its last legs, so to speak.

Liz could remember some wonderful times when the Rovers had played late into the night, until it had become a safety hazard owing to the amount of people who used to pile in for the live music. With all those feet tapping, they often expected it to collapse under the excitement.

After Liz had dropped Barnie off at home she climbed into her trusty van only to find that Ben had filled her tank with petrol. She sat for a moment and thought how kind he had been. He had saved her from the most horrendously long and tiring walk home in the pitch dark and the rain. Then collected her van, walked her dog, and what had she done in return? Nothing, she thought, attempting to convince herself that offering a man a bed for the night was the least she would do for anyone.

This was in case Nigel found out that Ben had spent the night – not that he should, of course. However, with the likes of Mrs Mangle in the village, anything could happen. So while Liz was still convincing herself that she had been simply being a Good Samaritan, still feeling unconvinced by her own personal explanation, she walked into the village hall to face Nigel's thunderous expression.

Oh God, this is not going to be easy, Liz thought to herself while putting on a cheery smile. She casually said to everyone present, "Sorry I'm late, folks, I got held up."

Nigel made a beeline for Liz, his face becoming darker, if that were possible, as he approached her. Then in a stage whisper that no one in the room could have failed to hear, he ground out, "And where have you been? I've been ringing and ringing you for two days!"

"Nigel, I'm sorry…"

"You're sorry! I've been worried sick about you, and why haven't you answered my calls? Where exactly have you been?"

"Nigel, if you give me a chance to get a word in, I'll tell you."

Liz waited, giving a haughty pause, attempting to make Nigel feel he had gone too far and he should allow her to speak without jumping down her throat. When Liz judged her pause had had the desired effect, she explained that on Friday evening she'd had to stay later at the big house she was working on because the owner was moving in on the Saturday.

"I must have left my phone in the van because Tom also rang me and, as I explained to him, I was so exhausted when I got home I went straight to bed and, to be honest, I still haven't checked my phone. It's in the van now."

"Well, what about this morning? I rang your mobile and your cottage and I got no answer, so where have you been this morning? You knew we were painting the scenery today."

"Who is painting the scenery, Nigel?" Liz said with a slight steeliness in her voice, warning him that she also had a temper.

"I overslept this morning; I was so tired that I simply overslept, as I have been working so hard lately. Then I took Barnie on the common for a walk. After all, the poor beast spends his days indoors when I'm working and it's not very fair on him. So here I am. Now let's simply get on with what we have to do, shall we?"

Nigel wasn't satisfied but he could see that their overheated exchange was being overheard by the butcher, the baker and the candlestick maker so if they didn't want everyone and their granny to know all of their business, he had better put a brave face on it.

Liz didn't know which was worse, Nigel being angry or Nigel being smarmy. If he just acted normal he could be what some might call reasonable-looking. The problem was he was never normal; he was mostly overbearing, sometimes grovelly. At other times he was downright dictatorial and God only knew what he was like as a teacher.

Liz spent the remainder of the afternoon painting scenery, starry nights, sheep and shepherds for the younger children's nativity. Then for the adults the theme was Cinderella so she had to create something that looked like a grand ball on some previously painted hardboard. However, Liz was determined to get as far as she could as she had promised Isabel a day out and she was actually really in need of a little R & R herself.

Taking a casual glimpse every so often to see if Nigel had calmed down, Liz saw very little change until they all stopped for a coffee break before they went home. He seemed to have cheered up considerably and even attempted a smile when they all recounted what had been achieved so far. As Liz painted for a living and not a hobby she had been able to crack on and even Nigel was pleased with her efforts. Of course, all the other helpers thought it so professional, saying how these were going to be the best pantomimes ever. Which, of course, they said every year. However, it really was coming together nicely and as far as Liz was concerned she was finished.

Foolish woman, thought Liz, I should have kept my thoughts to myself. Liz had just been patting herself on the back, thinking she was free of her duties, when Nigel started his clipboard round-up of what was still left to do and to whom it would be allocated. It was decided that costumes were the next most important item on the agenda, as various people began to drift away in wise little groups saying they needed to wash cups and sweep floors – anything, in fact, so that they were out of Nigel's line of vision.

Nigel swung round, catching Liz off guard. He looked directly at her saying, "Charity shops."

"Yees…"

"They are a great source of old clothes, curtains and sheets and things. You could look there. As you have a sewing machine, it wouldn't take much to alter them. I'll get Celia to give you some sizes and numbers, you know, how many shepherds and ball gowns et cetera. Right that's that, ermm."

And after delivering an earth-shattering blow once again, filling up any spare time that Liz could possibly have had in the coming weeks, Nigel walked off leaving Liz speechless. She would have liked to have argued, saying she simply didn't have enough spare time as it was, but on balance the fact that Nigel had seemed to have forgotten his earlier annoyance was at least something less to worry about.

As they closed the village hall she thanked God Nigel had taken his own car, which meant that Liz wouldn't have to share a car with him, which in turn would have meant giving him another chance to interrogate her on her missing hours. Tom would go mad if he knew how much control Nigel appeared to have over Liz.

To be honest, it wasn't that he had any control. It was that Liz sometimes found being on her own since Tom went away to university a little bit lonely. Therefore she didn't mind the odd curry night in or the odd drink at the Dog and Duck on a night when the group wasn't playing.

However, Nigel did seem to read more into it than just company, and Liz felt a little guilty at times because as far as she was concerned there was no way she would ever marry again. She could never be as lucky again in her lifetime, to find another soul mate as she had with Bob.

"See you later," Nigel called out of his car window as Liz climbed into her little van, hoping to make a speedy escape. “I’ll bring an Indian and a bottle of wine, make it about seven thirty, okay?”

Unable to think of an excuse, she smiled and called back, “Yes, see you then.”

As she drove her little van back home in the darkness she felt uneasy. She knew she shouldn’t keep allowing Nigel to think that they were ‘an item’ when all the time she knew that, if she were totally honest with herself, sometimes he really irritated her. He wasn’t bad-looking, he was about five feet eight tall, very slim, sandy-coloured hair and blue eyes, with a very nondescript dress code. Liz thought that was probably something to do with his job as a maths teacher – he was probably expected to wear bland tan-coloured V-neck sweaters with matching corduroys and a plaid shirt underneath. Always with a tie, and actually Liz could swear it was a knitted tie, which actually made her cringe.

“Now I’m just being cruel, and that’s not fair,” Liz said into the darkness of the van.

He had a nice face, when he chose to smile. Liz was really struggling to find any points about Nigel that she really found pleasant. He wasn't like that at the beginning, surely? she thought. He was good company, I'm sure he was. He'd been a comfort to her when she'd felt lost after Bob died and she had been glad to have the company.

But, she thought to herself, was that all it was – company? Yes, because Nigel quite often became a little amorous after a couple of glasses of wine and attempted to kiss Liz with intent; and his intentions manifested themselves with him pressing himself against her while pushing his mouth firmly to herd as though she was a kiss of life dummy. And it actually made Liz feel nauseated. The first time it happened she blamed the takeaway and the wine; however, he now made attempts to carry it out while saying goodnight, and there were only so many times Liz could accidentally turn away at the same time, enabling him to kiss her on the cheek instead.

For some odd reason and out of the blue, Ben Paris's face popped into her head and she found herself idly wondering what it would be like to be kissed by him.

Chapter 8

Nigel arrived at seven fifteen, which was another thing that kind of bugged Liz – he was always early. That sounded trite even to her own ears when she muttered to herself from upstairs as he let himself into her cottage, shouting his arrival. Yes, it was nice she thought, for a man to be on time, but when she thought she had another fifteen minutes to dress casually she hated being caught off guard, which Nigel always did.

"Get a grip," Liz told herself, "you're simply nit-picking now, which is not very nice as Nigel's come round and brought a takeaway and a bottle of wine and never asks for anything in return…" Well, except, she thought to herself, a necking session at the front door as he left, which she was finding more and more unpleasant. Liz decided that it was all very unfair of her. She was going to have to have a serious talk with herself about her relationship with Nigel. And when she finally came to the conclusion, which she knew she would in the end, she must tell him. It wasn't fair of her to keep him thinking that at some point they would end up in bed, as most couples would have by now.

She knew Nigel had been giving her space since Bob died. But she also knew that he was unsure of his ground with her as she had loved Bob very much and could never imagine being with anyone else. Liz could smell the Indian and knew that Nigel would be in the kitchen busily plating it up. They could never eat out of the cartons as she had done when Bob was alive and as she still did when Tom was home, in front of a roaring fire. It all had to be done correctly and they would eat at the kitchen table in a civilised manner. Another of Nigel's pet hates was meal sharing, whereas when Liz and Bob used to buy a takeaway they would get a selection of meals and just dip in. Nigel was quite disgusted when Tom was home once and he suggested it.

"Mmm, smells nice, Nigel. I can't wait. I can't remember when I last ate – a slice of toast before taking Barnie on the common, I think. Oh, you've laid the table, great…"

"Yes, I thought we would have our meal then snuggle up in front of the fire. I've put some logs on for you as it was almost out when I arrived."

"Mmm, yes, I didn't have time as I just came in and went straight into a hot bath. I was frozen from painting in the village hall. But at least that's me done, except for the costumes, which I simply don't know when I'm going to find the time to source and make, Nigel."

"What do you mean, you're finished? You have backdrops for Cinderella; you've got the kitchen scene, the bedroom scene with the two ugly sisters; and… Well, I can't think at the moment as I haven't got my clipboard with me, but you're by no means finished."

Nigel may as well have added "my girl" at the end of the sentence.

He had stopped eating with his fork halfway from food to mouth, but after delivering his little speech he put his fork into his mouth quite forcefully. Liz actually hoped he would choke on it at that precise moment. Well, she thought, she might as well tell him now that next Saturday was spoken for. Then he would have a week to chew it over.

"Oh, well, to be honest, Nigel, I thought with it simply being a village production and not an am-dram, the background scenery I painted the other day would have been enough."

"Well, if you just want a simple pantomime thrown together, fair enough, but I thought we wanted a pantomime to be proud of. Well, that was my impression. However…"

"Look, no one is saying we don't want to be proud of it, Nigel, but it is only a village pantomime. It's meant for fun; it s not a professional production."

Liz was trying to choose her words carefully so as not to upset him any more than she couldn't avoid, as she could see the little pulse at the side of his neck begin to throb, which was a sure sign that he was about to blow a gasket.

"But, Nigel, I have my job to do and I have only a certain amount of time to myself…"

"Oh, I see, you're saying you're the only one with a job? I'm sorry; I was under the impression that I was the one with the career as a mathematics teacher."

"No, Nigel, that's not what I'm saying, only you know that I play at the Dog and Duck on Tuesdays and Thursdays and I have a full workload on at the moment at the sheltered as everyone wants their decorating done before Christmas. I'm not saying I don't want to help – I'm just saying that I think doing all those extra backdrops is a bit, well, unnecessary for a village performance."

After she finished speaking she waited with a fork full of rice for the explosion, but it was worse. Generally, Nigel either exploded or gave you the silent treatment. The silent treatment made you feel even worse, as he would give an impression of a wounded dog. This meant that you actually became desperate to give him what he wanted, just to ease the tension.

“I see, so the Dog and Duck is more important than the village pantomime? That’s fine, don’t you worry. I’ll try to get someone else to paint the backdrops. I know the group is more important to you than anything else.”

“Nigel, that is not what I’m saying. I’m saying—”

“It’s all right, you don’t have to explain. I know you like to play in your little group. I’ll try to find someone else.”

Liz was really irritated now, but she had to stay calm or this could turn quite bad. Nigel was impossible when he got the lip on and you ended up doing more than he asked for in the first place just to cheer him up.

“Nigel. I will do the backdrops, but I’m not sure when. It can’t be next Saturday – I’ve promised Isabel I will go shopping with her. I can’t break my promise, as I haven’t had time to see her properly for ages and she is my best friend. But,” Liz managed to jump in as she could see Nigel was gearing up to make an objection, “I could probably do them in the evening if you give me the key to the village hall. Unless, of course, it will be open for one reason or another. It won’t matter to me as I will be out the back painting. Soooooo,” Liz rushed on before Nigel could interrupt, “you want a kitchen scene, a bedroom scene complete with ugly sisters, and that’s the lot? Because, Nigel, that has to be it, as I’ll have lots of last-minute decorating work to do plus the group, which I won’t stop doing no matter how busy I am. You know how much I love the group nights,” Liz said emphatically so as to show that he had pushed his luck as far as he could by attempting to belittle the group.

"No, no, that's fine, I'm almost sure," he said. Then, giving her a wary look, he appeared to decide he had better make it enough. He did try to make small talk but it was rather stilted. Then after he had finished his meal and two stiff glasses of wine he made the suggestion that she must be tired and he would let her get off to bed. Liz was glad he hadn't attempted one of his amorous sessions at the front door, as she was in no mood to have fended him off.

Feeling too wound up for sleep, she decided to fetch her torch, put her wellies and her old warm dog-walking coat on, and take Barnie out for a stroll, which always helped her relax. Barnie was at the door before she could button up her coat.

Chapter 9

Liz had an early start at the Mill where she was about to start painting Angus's mother's bedroom. She lived in one of the self-contained flats that had once formed part of the Old Mill, but that had been renovated into sheltered accommodation, suitable for thirty tenants. The renovation had been the brain child of the village solicitor and the very first inhabitant had been the solicitor's own mother.

Liz felt as though she lived there herself sometimes. Once one tenant had brought her in to decorate, the smell of the paint seemed to tempt the others into being redecorated, whether it needed it or not. It occurred to Liz that they enjoyed the company of someone being in the flat and it gave them a new outlook, choosing colours and curtains.

Angus had asked Liz if she could simply freshen up his mother's bedroom as she had been ill recently. He'd told her, "If she has to look at those walls for one more day she thinks she'll go mad."

Arriving bright and early meant in theory that Liz would have an early finish. However, it rarely worked like that. There was always one little job that had nothing to do with decorating that Liz always felt she simply must do for the client before she left.

Iona McLaughlin was a tall woman, which was where Angus had inherited his stature. It was sad to see how she had begun to shrink as she'd got older. However, she was still a force to be reckoned with if crossed, although Liz knew her bark was worse than her bite and took absolutely no notice of her blustering. Iona had known Liz since she was a bairn, she would say, so she had no secrets from her. She had seen her marry and seen her widowed.

The morning flew past as Liz worked steadily, only stopping when Iona insisted she did for a bite of lunch. Liz knew that this was all part of the decorating, the company and the gossip; this was where she would be asked about daily life in the village. Who was still married to whom or who had divorced. It was rare that she was asked who had passed away as elderly people seemed to have radar where that was concerned. They may never have left the building yet they always knew who had died.

Liz got on very well with all of the residents and was highly thought of. It was well known that in cases of an emergency Liz would help. She often nipped to the chemist if anyone needed medicines or the corner shop if they ran out of something that their family had forgotten to bring. However, there was an unwritten agreement that the residents didn't take advantage of Liz's good nature.

Liz finished the bedroom and was just folding her dust sheets, making sure she left the room as tidy as she had found it, particularly in mind of their various disabilities. Packing her things away, she could hear Iona in her little bathroom, talking away to herself, “I know I had more tablets. I can’t understand it.”

“Hey, you okay in there? I can hear you muttering. Can I help?”

“I know that I had enough painkillers, Angus got a new prescription just the other day, yet I can’t for the life of me find them. Do me a favour with your young eyes – will you look in this cabinet and see if you can find them?”

Iona told Liz the name of the painkillers, and that the box was oblong and red, and she was sure she had put it in the corner next to her blood pressure tablets. But it was clear that they were not there.

“Nope, I’m afraid not, Iona. Listen, can I go and get you some? It won’t take long and I don’t mind.”

“Oh bother, I feel awful asking you to do that after you’ve worked so hard all day, but I do need them or I won’t be able to move by tomorrow when Angus comes. He normally gets them for me… I'm sure he got them just the other day when he came… I would be so grateful, Liz, if you don't mind. Just ask McLeish, he won't mind."

Mr McLeish was the village chemist who knew everyone by their various illnesses. He would go out of his way to help, and was simply known as McLeish. It was still only three o'clock so Liz had plenty of time and she would still be finished early. She had got it into her head that when she got home she was going to make a Christmas cake, so she would get the ingredients from the little shop next door to the chemist rather than drive to the supermarket. So her trip to the chemist, as she explained to Iona, wasn't out of her way after all.

Someone had been making a Christmas cake in the Mill and the smell had been so delicious while Liz was painting that she had become determined to make her own this year instead of being lazy and buying one as she had done for the last couple of years. She always used to make her own cake, and Tom would insist on helping. He would stir the cake, as he had more elbow power than Liz, then as a treat would clean the bowl until there was hardly a trace left to wash.

Liz had forgotten how much pleasure she got from sorting out her ingredients for the cake, lining the tin… Then the smell as she added all the different fruits that she had hurriedly soaked in hot water. At one time she would have soaked her fruit over night but her spur of the moment decision to make her cake today meant she would have to cut corners. It wouldn't matter just this once, Liz thought to herself as she placed the cake very carefully into the centre of her oven and closed the door gently. Checking the time, she knew the cake wouldn't be ready until…oh, possibly ten-ish.

It was after she had washed up and was carrying her well-earned coffee through to the cosy little sitting room that Liz saw the scrap of paper that had been pushed through the door. As she picked it up from the doorstep she knew instantly what it was about and she tutted loudly to herself.

“Oh no, bloody meeting, I’d forgotten all about that. Well, I’m not going. I’ve got my cake in the oven now and that’s that.”

Liz was still muttering to herself when her phone rang, then thought how amazing it was that the minute you made yourself a coffee the phone or the doorbell rang.

“Hi, no, well, yes, I’ve just picked it up. Actually I’d forgotten and I’ve just put my Christmas cake in the oven, so I’m not coming.”

Liz was attempting to get out of going to the village hall meeting, about the proposal of the building of a new village hall. The meetings were long and boring and they never got any further than talking about it because there wasn’t enough money. Even if they had a hundred bingo nights and a hundred jumble sales, which they had on a regular basis as it was, there was still no way there would be enough to build a new hall.

"Liz, you have to come. I'm not going on my own, and I met Niiigel in the village and I promised that we would both be there," Isabel cajoled. "Anyway, it seems it's the only time we ever get to see each other at the moment, as you never seem to be free."

Isabel spoke in such a way as to make Liz feel really guilty. "I know, I know, I'm sorry, you're right, but I've told Nigel that we are both going shopping on Saturday and that's final."

"Yes, he mentioned that, so beware – he will probably try to rope you into something concerning Saturday this evening."

"Oh no, I promise. I am so looking forward to simply wandering the shops and having lunch out and I need to keep my eye open for Christmas presents. No, he won't change my mind, but all right, I suppose I will have to go to the blasted meeting, but they are soooo boring, Isabel. It won't make a jot of difference whether I'm there or not, and, as you say, it just means I am within hollering distance of all those extra little jobs he finds for me to do. But no matter what happens, I must be back for ten o'clock."

"Why? Is that when you turn into a pumpkin? Ha ha."

"No, you idiot, that's when my Christmas cake comes out of the oven."

"What's the matter with good old Tesco's Christmas cakes anyway? And who on earth's going to eat it – you hate Christmas cake."

"Funny that, you're right. Well, I don't hate it – I can't resist the smell – but it is a little heavy for me, so I'll probably give it to Tom to take back to uni. He'll eat anything and his flatmates are the same, so it will be well appreciated. I just felt the need to be domesticated, like I used to be… When Bob was alive and Tom was young."

Chapter 10

The car park at the village hall was almost full, meaning that the hall would be full. Nigel would be presiding over the meeting as usual and she would be expected to take her place in the front row, as usual. However, as she was with Isabel and there were no seats left in the front row, they sat in the middle leaning against the radiator so at least they wouldn't freeze for a change.

Liz suddenly made an involuntary sound, which Isabel's perfect hearing detected. She looked enquiringly into her friend's face.

"What? What? Tell me." Isabel was always quick to detect a little bit of gossip and couldn't wait for Liz to spill the beans.

"In the front row, but keep your voice down… The guy with the Hugh Grant hair… That's Ben Paris, and, erm, I don't know who that is with him."

"It must be his girlfriend because the grapevine says he's not married. Mmm, he's nice. You didn't say how nice. She's niiice too, I suppose, if you go for that type," Isabel said in a catty voice, while attempting to describe Ben's woman friend impartially, however unsuccessfully.

"I wonder what he's doing here is more to the point," Liz said, trying to sound only vaguely interested, but failing miserably. Isabel could detect the stirrings of interest from her best friend that had been absent since Bob had died.

The meeting droned on as predicted, but eventually the committee began to talk about finance, which was when Liz and Isabel almost nodded off to sleep with the sheer excitement of it all…not. Match funding was mentioned once more, whereby if the 'new village hall' committee raised X amount of money then various institutes such as banks and building societies in the surrounding areas would agree to match the amount, helping to reach the final goal faster.

"That's all very well," another member of the committee chimed in, "but then you have to spend a chunk of that money on such things as land searches, architects' fees and so on and so on, until half of what you have worked really hard to find has gone."

It was at that point when Isabel and Liz began to slide nicely into that state of oblivion where you don't actually hear the words being spoken, only the tone, very much like being in church. All of a sudden they realised that someone in the front row had actually stood up and was talking. Liz sat to attention and strained to hear what was being said.

"Mr speaker, my name is Ben Paris and I have just moved into Juniper Manor. I am, as some may know, an architect and my practice is in Edinburgh. And as a gesture of goodwill, as I am now resident in this village and have a vested interest, I would like to offer my services free of charge."

There was an astounded round of applause and lots of muttering among those in the audience who had attended these meetings for the last five years and had never heard anyone give anything for nothing. Liz and Isabel looked at each other in amazement then Isabel shoved Liz with her elbow, indicating she should take a look at Ben Paris's lady friend. The woman sitting next to Ben was far from pleased – to say she seemed shocked would be an understatement. The only indication that she had actually heard Ben's announcement was the very unenthusiastic tap of her hands together while looking utterly astounded, and not at all happy.

As the general clapping and euphoria calmed down and Nigel called the meeting to order once again, it was obvious that he could barely contain himself. After a very, very – for Nigel – brief end to the meeting, complete with the most spectacular grovelling thank you to Mr Paris for his generosity, Nigel almost fell over himself clambering over to introduce himself personally to Ben and his partner.

Sometimes even Liz felt a little sick at Nigel's fawning nature when meeting someone whom he felt was important. She could see him introducing himself and could almost guess word for word what he would be informing the new couple. Isabel nudged Liz and they both intuitively began to shrink down and make for the door, attempting to join the throng of villagers departing, only to hear Nigel shouting for Liz to come and meet Ben and Fiona. He was saying it as though he had known them for years.

"Damn. Listen, I'm off. They won't need me."

"Oh no you're not. You made me come, so you are in it all the way. Anyway you can assess your competition – you never know, she may be moving into the village too."

The reluctant duo made their way towards the little group who were now standing alone as the hustle of minutes ago had died down very quickly. Nigel was waiting to introduce with a flourish Ben and Fiona to Liz and Isabel.

"Ben, Fiona, this is Liz Cassidy, my, er… Our village decorator, ha ha. She does all our scenery and things for our village plays and pantomimes. And this is Isabel Eskdale, erm, Liz's friend from school, also a resident of our little village. Liz, Isabel, this is Mr Paris, er, Ben and his partner Fiona. They are both architects."

It obvious to see that Nigel was totally in awe of Fiona being not only a female but a fully qualified architect to boot, a fact he seemed to find astonishing. He was totally enthralled – his eyes were drawn towards Fiona's dark and what could only be described as brooding eyes, with their long, black lashes. Her hair was hidden beneath an Elizabeth Taylor type fur hat, which gave her an air of Lara from *Dr Zhivago*. Liz could see with amusement that Nigel was almost drooling over her mystery and beauty. He found it almost impossible to keep track of the conversation while Ben was saying hello again to Liz.

Liz was grateful that Nigel was distracted. She nervously held her breath to hear what

Ben Paris would come out with. Isabel was watching the interchange of unspoken undercurrents with great pleasure. She knew instantly that she and Fiona would not like each other. She had no idea if they would ever come across each other socially but she knew she was competition, which she didn't want. She felt a distinct spark between her best friend and Ben Paris, though. Thank goodness! At least Niiigel could never compete with Mr Paris, thought Isabel.

"Hello again, er, Mr Paris."

"Ben, please. Surely we know each other well enough by now? After all…"

"Yes, eh, Ben, yes of course. I hope you got moved in all right?"

As Ben held out his hand to shake Liz's it may have looked to any onlooker like a normal handshake and yet to Liz it felt like an electric shock, which almost made her snatch her hand from his warm firm grip. He seemed to take aeons to release her.

"Yes, thank you very much; and I hope you can find the time to finish the door handle and finger plate one day, when you're not painting scenery, of course," Ben said with a smile that covered a multitude of questions and innuendos. Liz looked at Nigel's face and she could see that he was already wondering what Ben had meant. Luckily he was so enthralled with whatever it was that Fiona was saying that the moment passed. Liz shook Fiona's hand, while Fiona looked slightly disdainfully down at Liz as though she were royalty being introduced to the workers.

Although, to be fair, everyone looked down on Liz as she was so small. Fiona's pained expression may have been simply that she was bored, or cold, or not well. Whatever, she obviously wanted to leave and she let Liz's hand drop and walked off in the direction of the door, with Nigel following like an adoring puppy.

Isabel had been making her own introductions to Ben Paris as no one else had offered and Isabel was no slouch in that direction. They seemed to be chatting easily, Isabel telling Ben that her best friend Liz was the hard worker around here and not simply the village decorator or the painter of scenery, as Niiigel had led him to believe. Liz, whose attention was back from watching Nigel doing his puppy thing, scoffed at Isabel's puffing up of her importance. Still worried at what might come out if the conversation resumed as to how Ben and she had met, Liz reminded Isabel that she had to be home by ten.

"Oh yes, if she doesn't get home by ten she is like Cinderella herself and she'll turn back into the scullery maid instead of the best fiddler in the county."

"Hush, you. Take no notice of her," Liz said awkwardly, feeling a little provincial at the mention of hurrying home to take a cake out of the oven, not to mention the fiddle playing. What on earth must the poor man be thinking? Cakes, fiddles, village halls, God, how domestic could you get?

"I've got a Christmas cake in the oven, that's all, and I need to get back before it burns. So it was lovely meeting you both, but I must be off," Liz said while backing away towards her little van before Nigel could detach himself from his new attraction. But Ben wasn't in such a hurry to let her go and appeared to be enjoying her slight discomfort.

"You play the fiddle? What, just at home or in an orchestra or something?"

"She plays in the best folk group in these parts. Believe me, you would love it. You should go to the Dog and Duck on a Tuesday or a Thursday – you'll have a great night."

"I might just do that, and I meant it about you coming to the house to finish off a few things for me, but only when you have the time," Ben said with a mischievous smile in his eyes that hinted at more than doorknobs.

"Yes, yes, I'll do that, I promise."

Liz was backing away towards her van and called to Nigel that she had to go…cake in the oven…et cetera. Both she and Isabel climbed into the van and waved as they passed the trio still talking. Well, Nigel was still doing the talking. Ben and Fiona looked as though they couldn't escape fast enough.

Liz and Isabel were busily making their escape like Bonnie and Clyde, hoping that Nigel wouldn't notice until they had safely made their getaway. Ben gave a wry grin as they flew past him, as though he understood perfectly. They were sat around Liz's kitchen table with a steaming cup of coffee before they stopped laughing.

"It's not funny, Isabel, he won't be best pleased, and you know who'll get it in the neck and it won't be you."

"Oh for goodness' sake, Liz, when are you going to tell him to sling his hook? He uses you, takes up all your spare time and… Well, he's a pain in the…you know what."

“I know, I know, but he was very kind when Bob died and I was at a bit of a loss. He sort of gave me so much to do it kind of took my mind off being alone again. There is something to be said for that, but I know what you mean. I’m finding it harder and harder to actually have a sensible conversation with him any more. I’ve realised he simply wants to organise things, not only me but everything and anything.

“What he needs is a large project – you never know, the new village hall may just be it. He may end up so involved in planning and organising that he won’t have time to, well, interfere in my life.”

“You mean pester you, or try to take over your life, or stop you having any fun. But you’re right, this may just be the diversion you need. After all, you are not a builder, although if he had his way you would be sent away to learn. The thing is, now that there is a definite possibility of outside help in the form of the architect’s plans without any cost involved, and match funding and so forth, this may just take off.”

Chapter 11

Bright and early Monday morning Liz was back at the Mill decorating a bathroom for old Minnie, Iona's neighbour, and then she had a lounge to do farther down the corridor later on in the week. In fact Liz had so much continuous work within the Mill she would never have to advertise.

She finished the tiny bathroom early, so Liz thought now was as good a time as any to call in at Ben's and finish off the door handle. It couldn't take her more than half an hour. She was a little nervous about going back, although she had no idea why.

Part of her was very curious to see if Fiona actually lived at the Manor or if she had simply stayed for the weekend to help Ben settle in. It had nothing whatsoever to do with her, though she couldn't help but be curious. For some reason they just didn't seem a likely pair, although, again, what did she know? She had lost touch with life, well, real life, when Bob had died and she had been quite happy to opt out of social involvement full stop. That was apart from the Rovers, which kept her sane.

She parked her little van and walked up to the freshly painted, large Victorian wooden door. She admired her own handiwork, thinking how very smart it looked, under the portico that covered the immediate area where you were likely to get wet or wind-blown. Lifting the brass knocker she gave a rap at the door that sounded far more confident than she felt.

It was obvious to Liz that Ben was surprised to see her standing there, and she began to feel very uncomfortable, under his intense gaze. She had forgotten all about her normal working clothes, which consisted of dungarees and work boots. Feeling a little self-conscious she began to pluck at her jacket while wiping her boots on the doormat.

Ben was clearly pleased to see her after his initial surprise, almost hauling her in mid wipe of her boots.

"Well, hello, what a nice surprise on a dull Monday."

Liz felt slightly less uncomfortable about just dropping in without letting him know. However she became more conscious about her dress when eyeing his casual attire from head to foot. He certainly looked a lot different to the previous times they had met. And he made jeans look as though they were made for him, those and his zip-up jacket over an open shirt.

Liz dragged her gaze away towards the floor as she suddenly realised she was about to blush at being caught checking him out…as Isabel would have said.

"I thought I would call in and finish the door handle and finger plate, if that's convenient for you, err…?"

"Ben. When will you simply call me Ben? We are friends, I hope. After all, I slept in your son's bed and took your horse for a walk, now, didn't I?"

"You did, you certainly did, but for goodness' sake don't say that in front of Nigel or he'll have a canary."

"Oh I see. Nigel is your boyfriend then?"

"No, no, he isn't. He is a friend. Well, he has been a good friend since my husband died three years ago."

"I'm terribly sorry, I shouldn't have pried into your affairs."

"Oh that's all right, you weren't to know; although after you've been in the village for about a month you will know everything there is to know about everyone. It's that kind of village, so if you have any secrets you are embarrassed about, forget it."

Liz had managed to lighten the conversation away from Bob and herself and on to general topics. Ben noticed that Liz had attempted to make him feel at ease and carried on in the same vein.

“So, am I the topic of village gossip at the moment?”

“Put it this way, no one but me and the builders have been inside this house, yet they know what colours you have chosen for each room. And before long they will know every piece of furniture you have delivered. Don’t forget the removal people and builders have to live somewhere.”

Ben laughed but even he wasn’t sure if he wanted everyone to know everything about him just yet. Although wasn’t that why he had moved to a small community, to become part of something instead of just one of many in the city?

“Can I get you a coffee before you start, or are you in a hurry? I realise this is not a social call and you’re working.”

Liz was just about to refuse and make her usual fast getaway, when, for some reason, she stopped, saying yes, she would love that…before giving herself time to change her mind.

They made their way to the kitchen, which Liz knew very well, but of course it looked much more lived in now than when she had decorated it. It was wonderfully warm and pleasant, considering it was pretty horrible outside. And she wondered if Fiona was responsible for the homely touches and splashes of colour from the toaster, the kettle and the coffee machine, not to mention all the deep red accessories giving the room a modern and homely feel.

Ben lifted the lid on the bright red Rayburn and put the kettle on as they talked, all the while seemingly very used to catering for visitors even if it was to simply make coffee.

"I've never really had a chance to thank you for the excellent work you have done in my home. In fact we haven't really had a chance to talk.

"I have a confession to make. The first time I met you, I actually thought… Well, I thought that you must be the apprentice as you seemed too young to be the actual decorator. I hope you're not offended?"

"No, don't worry, you're not the first to think that. It's because I am so short – people assume I'm younger. However, on second sight they soon realise I'm a lot older, I'm afraid."

Liz carried on before he felt he had to refute how old she looked to him on second sight.

"I, err, really, really enjoyed working on your home. It was so refreshing to work on a project that wasn't to simply emulsion and refresh plasterboard walls. I shouldn't say that, as that type of work is my bread and butter. But it makes such a difference working on a project where the building has such character, where craftsmen have carved arches and cornices and not simply bought them at the DIY shop. You must know what I mean – after all, you're an architect and you must come across such wonderful buildings every day."

As Liz looked up for Ben's reply she realised that he was staring at her and she blushed before he said quickly to ease her embarrassment, "I know exactly what you mean; it's just, I don't know why I should have thought this, but I never realised how passionate you were about your work. As I say, I don't know why that should surprise me in any way but it does. I suppose nowadays I meet such a lot of developers and renovators who simply want to slap on the paint and tart a property up so they can rent it out or resell quickly. So to meet someone like myself who derives such pleasure from the actual architecture is so refreshing."

"Ha, you have no idea how much pleasure I had working on something that didn't wobble when you screw something into it. Most of the modern properties that I work on I have to be so careful when replacing door handles in case I actually screw through the hardboard door because they are hollow inside."

Liz laughed, saying that's why she had been loath to damage his door with a screwdriver the night she'd got stuck in the bathroom. When Liz mentioned that night they both took one look at each other and burst out laughing.

"You have no idea what a bloody shock I got when you shot up into a sitting position in the bath."

"And you have no idea what a shock I got, when you flew in through the door. I was so tired; I still cannot believe how on earth I could have fallen asleep in an empty house in the bath, with nothing but a dust sheet to keep me warm. Then, as if that wasn't bad enough, I had to go and run out of petrol. I thought you were a kerb crawler, you know? But instead of being frightened, to be honest, I was so fed up that if you had turned out to be a creep you would have got a mouthful, I can tell you. The spotty youth at the petrol station didn't know how lucky he was to be locked inside his protective bubble either."

"Ha ha, I was right the first time, you are a spitfire. God help the person who makes you angry after a bad day at the office."

"I'm not normally, I had just had a belly full by the time you picked me up, and don't ever repeat that the way it sounds. Especially not to anyone vaguely related to anyone within a fifty mile radius of this village."

"And especially not to Nigel, I gather? Who I'm presuming doesn't know I spent the night at your house?"

"Oh God, no, especially not to Nigel. And actually not even to Tom, my son, unless there is no alternative."

They both burst out laughing at the thought of Nigel being outraged. Ben didn't even know Nigel yet he had guessed already the type of person he was after their first meeting. Nigel had a way of ingratiating himself with people he met and he had no idea how obvious he was. A crueller person than Liz would have described him as a Uriah Heep type of person. Even his handshake made you feel a little uneasy.

"Don't get me wrong – give Nigel a project such as the new village hall and a clipboard and he'll work his socks off… Well, more to the point, he will organise everyone to work *their* socks off."

Again they laughed simultaneously, as they both recognised those types of people from all walks of life, not just Juniper Green.

"The problem with being a decorator is that I tend to get roped into little odd jobs for people so I have become a kind of jack of all trades but master of none, as they say."

"Why do I get the feeling that Nigel takes advantage of your generous nature?"

"Well, to be honest, most of my work actually comes from the old Mill, our sheltered accommodation. It has thirty flats, well, twenty-nine – one of them is occupied by the on-site scheme manager, or warden as she is sometimes called. I swear once one person has something decorated they all smell the paint and I'm there for months. I don't mind at all. I like all the oldies, they are people I've grown up with. They have watched me grow up and I've watched them grow older. However, I tend to put fuses into plugs, bulbs into lights and tighten loose doorknobs… Speaking of which, I should really be getting on with yours."

"Yes, I'm sorry, I mustn't keep you just because I've finished for the day. But it's been very nice chatting to you. Normally when I'm working in the office in Edinburgh I never lift my head. Fiona will tell you I'm a workaholic. My intention is to work much less. I intend to take on fewer projects but more interesting work, instead of, as you say, the bread and butter work. I will, of course, occasionally still work in Edinburgh, but the idea is that eventually I will work completely from home."

As they walked up towards the fateful bathroom that Liz remembered only too well, she commented that she hoped all the windows were shut this time. They laughed again simultaneously, which was nice, then Ben diverted Liz to a room at the front of the house where she remembered the sun had shone brightly in at midday when she had painted it.

“This is my office.” he said proudly and showed her into the newly furnished room. Liz stood just inside the door while Ben moved forward, showing off his wonderful mixture of modern, contemporary and antique furniture. The mix was eclectic yet it worked perfectly. His desk was clearly an antique yet the chair looked sumptuously contemporary and was probably ergonomically designed to support his back while working for hours at a drawing board. His drawing board was placed at the large window, obviously to catch the light at certain times of the day. As his chair was on castors it worked perfectly.

A sumptuous cream leather sofa was situated across the corner and an armchair of chocolate brown leather was arranged around a beautiful glass occasional table at an angle, providing a comfortable and relaxing space for when he were not working. Liz was totally impressed, which pleased Ben as he had designed the interior and felt duly proud of his achievements. There was, of course, the usual office equipment; however, it seemed to melt into the background, giving the room a look of comfort and opulence.

"Wow, you certainly know how to make yourself comfortable, I see. No wobbly desk and chair for you. Our home office, which was Bob's, Tom uses now when he is home. It consists of an old desk we bought at an auction and an old captain's chair on wheels, which I recovered, and it's all pushed into the corner of the small bedroom. This is gorgeous. I absolutely love your choice of furniture – how brave of you to put such a mix together? And it works perfectly. I bet Fiona helped you choose it?"

"Actually no, she didn't. I like to choose my own furnishings. After all, I am the one who is going to live with them. And we have such different tastes. She likes throw-away furniture so she can change it long before it wears out. I choose every piece carefully as I intend it to last for life."

The way Ben said that gave Liz a slight thrill. She had no idea why, but she totally and completely agreed with his sentiment. After admiring the room for a little longer, Liz sighed, saying she would have to make a start on the door as Barnie would be desperate for a walk by the time she got home.

It took twenty minutes, if that, to complete the handle and finger plate, and as she left the house Ben thanked her, adding, "Phew, now I can use the bathroom without worrying that I might get stuck in there without anyone to rescue me."

As they laughed together about the now infamous door handle joke, he reminded her that she was always welcome.

Liz simply smiled, knowing she would never go uninvited when the whole idea of him furnishing an office was to work. She should have warned him that a carelessly given invitation in a village could turn out to be pretty disastrous when working from home. However, he would soon find that out for himself.

Chapter 12

After taking Barnie for his walk or mad half hour running around the common in the pitch dark, Liz and Barnie made their way back home only to see Nigel's car parked outside. He wasn't in the car, which meant he had let himself into the cottage, which was another thing that was beginning to rankle with Liz. When had that all started? She had given him a key only at his insistence in case she went away on a holiday or in case she needed to ask him to feed Barnie. But as Nigel didn't really like Barnie and was always busy when the need arose, it was rather pointless him having a key.

A little ruffled around the edges even before she got into the cottage, Liz remonstrated with herself, saying she would definitely have to find a reason to ask for her key back. There she was, warning Ben about guarding his privacy, and she should have known better. Liz went in through the kitchen door and was in the process of wiping Barnie's huge paws so that he didn't track mud through to the lounge when Nigel shouted through.

"You've been a long time… I've been waiting for you."

Liz ground her teeth in an attempt not to bite back by asking how he could possibly know she'd been a long time if even she hadn't known how long Barnie and she would want to stay out.

"Well, I decided Barnie needed a long run. After all, he's been in all day, you know."

"I don't know why you have a dog when you're working. He must eat a ton and cost a fortune."

"Sorry, what was that?" said Liz through gritted teeth. She had heard perfectly well but she just wanted to annoy him as he had annoyed her. Childish, she knew, but actually their relationship had become a little childish lately. Had she just noticed that or was it since she had met Ben? And was she in some way comparing the two men as actual male species? If so then Nigel was the proverbial wimp.

"I didn't expect you tonight, Nigel, to be honest. I was just about to stand in front of the fire and do a pile of ironing." Liz tried to make her night sound so boring that maybe he would take the hint and go home. But no, unfortunately nothing could put Nigel off when he was on a mission.

"Well, I came to bring you up to speed about the village hall. You know, you left the other night before we got a chance to talk about the wonderful news, about Ben and Fiona's generous offer of the architect's drawings and plans they are gifting to us… Well, the village. And since then I have been in touch with the main banks and building societies in town and they have agreed in principle to the match funding. After a rough calculation of the funding we have already and the promised funding we could receive, I actually think that I… I mean the village, could actually go ahead and make a start on the hall.

"Isn't that wonderful? I mean, can you just imagine what it will be like? Of course, I'll have to work very closely with Fiona, er…and Ben, naturally. But as she has already pointed out, I'll need some sort of survey to ask the villagers what they think, and what should be included in their village hall. I had to point out to her, as she is a newcomer, that, well, it doesn't do to give most of the villagers a choice, as most of them wouldn't know their a from their elbow, if you know what I mean."

"Yes, that is wonderful, Nigel, but I wouldn't get too carried away yet. There is a long way to go and I do think that Fiona is right. The villagers should all have an equal opportunity to make suggestions as to how the hall should be laid out.

"After all, before anything can go ahead you need to remind everyone what functions are carried out in the present hall. Then make decisions as to how those functions would fit into the new spaces, how it's going to be heated. Running costs differ with the sizes of halls, so if it were too big it would cost more to heat but if it were too small then you may wish you had made it larger. There is such a lot to discuss. You're right, you need to consult very closely with Fiona and the villagers.

"So please don't feel you have to find time for me, as I realise this is a very important project and you will be very heavily involved. You will have planning meetings, village meetings, and meetings with the parish council and power services, electric, gas and so on.

"Gosh, Nigel, you're going to be run off your feet, what with your job and marking and so forth. So hey, listen, as I don't have any of the skills you will require… You will need professionals, of course, so don't you worry yourself about me. I'll be kept busy with my little decorating business and my music, but maybe you had better give me my key back for the cottage. I may need to ask, erm… Mrs Mangle to let Barnie out occasionally if I can't make it home. You'll be far too busy with all your committee work to have to worry about him."

Nigel had been busily taking notes on all of Liz's suggestions so as not to forget anything. Liz could see he felt very important while he was taking notes. She could almost hear him saying to himself that she was right, that he was going to be a very busy [important] man and certainly wouldn't have time to nursemaid Liz or her mangy dog. In fact, he suddenly stood up saying, actually, he had an awful lot to do this evening so he had better be off. He mumbled that he needed to speak to Fiona – he would ring her when he got home as she had given him a card with her home and work numbers on. Yes, he had better get home and get on.

"Bye then, Liz, not sure when I'll see you. Possibly in the Dog and Duck one night. Bye."

Liz almost burst out laughing. She was about to close the front door on the swish of wind he'd caused as he fled out to his car. However, just as she was on the point of congratulating herself, he came dashing back. It got even better then – he had simply come back to give Liz her spare key. Then off he went again, this time without a word.

"Oh my God, I don't believe it. All it took was a dollop of importance with him at the head, and I'm rid of him. I know that sounds ungrateful and cruel, but, God, he is the absolute limit. I'm free. I can't believe it, I'm free. I must ring Isabel."

"You will never believe it" Liz went on to tell Isabel the story, still full of euphoria at the feeling that something heavy had been lifted from her shoulders.

"It's about bloody time; and for the next few weeks stay out of his way, because he will still be in the habit of giving you little jobs. He'll be looking in your direction to finish the panto for him as he now has bigger fish to fry. Ohhwa… Him and Fiona, hey, what do you think?"

"I think it's all in his head, but I think he really feels they made a connection and, to be honest, I hope they have. Do you know Isabel, I actually feel relieved. Is that wicked?"

"No, Liz, it is not wicked. He took you over, and everyone could see it but you. So be careful – you're not out of the woods yet. You are still handy to have around – most of his ideas came from you, but to hear him talk he thought of them first."

"He was kind to me after Bob died, but I really just want to spend time on my own now. I want to be my own boss, and I actually felt as though I had to answer to him. You know? As in where was I? Where had I been? What time would I be finished work, et cetera? Now I can take Barnie for a walk, have my takeaway in front of the fire again and enjoy my days off… Yippee!

"And wouldn't it be nice if Nigel and Fiona became an 'item'? Hee hee, Tom would love that. He hated coming home if he thought Nigel was going to be here, yet he never said anything to me. He was giving me space, I think, after Bob died, but I'm sure he was praying I wouldn't marry Nigel."

"Praying! He was on his knees, believe me. And you've no idea how much he disliked Niiigel. He often said so when we were at the Dog and Duck. He's a lovely lad, Tom, he would never have said anything in case it hurt you.

"You know, I might stir things… You know what? If I bump into Niiigel I will hint that, if he makes a good job of the village hall, they may name it after him, ha ha ha… Oh my God, he's just vain enough to believe it. Oh this is sooo brilliant and the more everyone piles the pressure on him the less time he is likely to bother you or, in turn, our days out. Get ready to shop until you drop, girl."

Chapter 13

Liz decided to give herself the day off as she had nothing urgent on until later in the week. She would enjoy her very rare morning doing whatever she chose to do. However, it wasn't in Liz's nature to laze around, so after enjoying a late breakfast she quickly donned her dog-walking clothes and took a very excited Barnie to the common.

It was cold and crisp with a watery sun – just the type of day to enjoy a brisk walk on the common and, in Barnie's case, a race around chasing imaginary hares. She was enjoying herself and suddenly realised that she had allowed herself to become bogged down, which had taken all her spontaneous free time away.

Tom had told her many times that she had no need to work full-time. Bob had left her comfortably off – the decorating was something she chose to do because she enjoyed it. How on earth had she ended up rushing from pillar to post doing all kinds of things that someone else was dictating she did?

She was so engrossed in her thoughts that she didn't at first notice, over at the far end of the common, a tall man in a dark coat throwing the ball for Barnie, who was chasing it with great gusto, almost knocking the stranger over when he carried it back to him. Liz made her way over towards the man and Barnie. As she got closer she recognised Ben's athletic frame.

"Hey, Mr, are you attempting to steal my horse?"

"Ha, I think the only way I would get him to come with me would be literally to ride him away. Morning, are you playing hooky today?"

"Well, yes, actually I am. I just decided to give myself the day off. I'm always getting into trouble with my son for working too much, so today is a holiday for Barnie and me. He thinks it's his birthday, being out during the day. I hate leaving him locked in all day, but needs must when I have work. He absolutely loves the common and very, very occasionally I take him to the beach. When I do, he is like a dog possessed. You should see him swim… I know, you would never think it of him.

“Anyway, what are you doing out? I thought you were going to work from home – this is not work. You must be so tempted to take the day off whenever you feel like it.”

“Actually no, I’ve always worked from my office in Edinburgh and my trouble was I would never take any time off at all. This move to the country is designed for me to work less and select only the work I enjoy for a change. I had a sudden urge to walk in the fresh air and I saw Barnie from my car. Two and two meant you had to be here somewhere, so I stopped. It must be nice, to have a dog to walk. It gives you a purpose, to be outside in the fresh air. I know, anyone can walk, but a man feels a little silly just walking alone. If you have a dog, well, it’s totally acceptable. Do you know what I mean?"

"Do you know, I've never thought about it before, but yes, I do know what you mean. Well, you can always take Barnie for a walk if ever you feel the need – he would be your friend for life if you did. Bob and I got Barnie ten years ago, and, of course, I didn't work then, so we walked every day. Now I feel very guilty sometimes, especially when he is left a long time. But I enjoy working – it keeps me in touch with people and I get a real kick out of decorating, would you believe?"

They walked round the common at least twice, throwing the ball in turn for Barnie while deep in conversation, before it became obvious that one or other of them would have to take their leave.

"The Rovers are playing tonight at the Dog and Duck if you're at a loose end, by the way. Any time after seven is good – you should get a seat if you drop in then."

"I may just do that. It's the fiddle you play, isn't it?"

"Yes, to my mother's horror. I was a violin student, turned fiddle player. But we all enjoy playing all different instruments. You'll enjoy it and I will introduce you to the other members of the group."

"Is Nigel a member of the group?"

"Nigel part of the group? Ha ha, definitely not. He doesn't think too much of the group, I'm afraid. He thinks of himself as more cerebral than musical. He doesn't care for the music nights much, though thankfully now he has a renewed interest in the village hall project, to keep him busy. Thanks to your very, very generous offer to donate your services for the new building."

Ben simply nodded with a knowing grin, as if to say he sensed relief on her part. Then they parted, him back to his car, which he had parked when he had spotted Barnie, and Liz through the cut and back towards her cottage with a very contented Barnie by her side.

Liz actually surprised herself sometimes. If she had met Ben Paris at a party or social function, she wouldn't have spoken to him much. Because although she wouldn't say she was shy, she didn't socialise very much apart from the regulars at the Dog and Duck, and, to be honest, she had known most of them since her school days so that was different. And she knew a lot of elderly people through her work, but people like Ben were not the type she would normally have anything to say to. On the whole it made her a bit tongue-tied and embarrassed. And yet, after her initial awkwardness while she was sat in his bath, she felt she had recovered very well and actually found him very easy to talk to.

Liz decided to have a long leisurely bath before choosing what she would wear this evening. It never normally crossed her mind to take care over the choice when she was playing, until this evening, that is. It was obvious to Liz that she was taking more care with her appearance because she rather hoped that Ben would call in and hear the group play. A man, she thought, who liked dogs and architecture must surely like music. If he did, then in her eyes he was all right.

She realised that if she wore her rather short red tartan kilt, a white short-sleeved blouse under her cranberry cardigan and black ribbed tights she would covered all the bases. The blouse so that she could remove her cardigan when it heated up in the pub; and the tights in case Angus lifted her up, as he usually did to the delight of the crowd. She didn't want to show everything she had. Her flat black pumps finished the ensemble – she always felt comfortable in those while her feet constantly tapped away to the fiddle music.

She was just having a coffee and settling Barnie before she left to meet up with Isabel, who lived almost on top of the Dog and Duck, when the phone rang. Liz's heart sank, because normally when the phone rang at this time of night it was Nigel.

However, a different voice on the other end shouted, “Can you hear me, Liz? Oh this connection is terrible, you would think I was in Australia instead of Benidorm. Oh hello, you’re there. I thought you might be at the Dog and Duck.”

“Hello, Mum, yes, I’m here, and yes, I was just on my way out. It’s group night, remember? How’s things with you?”

“Oh, Liz, you’ve no idea. You’ll never guess what…”

“Well, no, I won’t, mum, unless you tell me, how would I?”

“Well, saucy, I’m about to, aren’t I? You know Byron who lives in the next condo to mine? Well, he’s up and died.”

“Oh dear, I’m sorry to hear that.”

“Yes, but that’s not the worst of it. You know his friend Terry; well, he collapsed with a heart attack when the hospital said they couldn’t revive Byron.”

“No, they weren’t gay, Liz, they were just friends, ex pats, who came over more or less the same time. No, there was nothing funny about them, they were just friends. And now Frank and Mabel are talking about returning to England. They’re worried, if one or the other died, about what they would do on their own?

“Oh, Liz, things are changing over here. It’s not the same as it was, and, to be honest, the cost of living is going through the roof over here. I can remember when my pension went twice as far as it does now. For two pins I would come back myself, but oh, I don’t know, I gave up my flat and everything. And, to be honest, it’s winter over there and it’s still lovely here. Well, it’s not red hot, but nice, you know? We don’t have the fog or the frost or the snow. I don’t know if I could get used to that again, although I do miss the crisp winter mornings.”

“Mum, you’ve just had a shock and you feel a little lost without Byron and Terry. But I’m sure, once the summer comes back and you all lie like sardines in the sun, you’ll love it all over again. Listen, Mum, I have to go; I’m running late. But I’ll chat later on in the week, all right?”

“Yes, all right. Are you meeting Niiigel at the Duck?”

“Mum, you know Nigel doesn’t like to go to the Duck when we are playing, and, anyway, I’m not seeing as much of Nigel at the moment. He has a new project. I’ll tell you all about it later in the week, okay? Take care and try not to be too upset about your friends. I’m sure someone else nice will take on the condo – someone really gorgeous, ha ha. Bye for now, Mum.”

“Bye, dear, and I should be so lucky!”

Chapter 14

Liz arrived at Isabel's just as she was emerging from her cottage, which was a stone's throw from the Duck. This meant Liz could leave her little van outside and they would walk together.

"Wow, and what are you all dressed up for? Oh let me guess – you've got rid of Niiigel and decided to rejoin the human race. Or… Ohhwa, don't tell me Mr Paris is coming? Ohhwa, tell me more…"

"God, what are you like? I have no idea if Ben is coming."

"Ben… Oooh, it's Ben now, is it? Since when?"

"Honestly, before someone else leaks the news, I met Ben on the common this morning while walking the dog and mentioned that the group meets tonight and if he fancied a sing-song then to come. All right?

"And as for dressing up, I suddenly realised the only clothes he has seen me in are dungarees and dog-walking clothes. He must think I'm a right tramp in comparison to his lady friend Fiona."

"Mmm, you like him, don't you? I can tell. No, seriously, you look kind of happier than you have for ages. Honestly, Liz, you should have a bit of fun in your life. Niiigel has depressed you rather than helped you through your bereavement, in my opinion. But far be it from me to call him a pain in the bum – a pain in the bum…ha ha ha."

"I feel happier today for some reason, don't ask me why, but yes, I just felt like dressing up a little and 'rejoining the human race', as you so aptly put it. So look out world, here I come."

As they entered the Duck some of the group were busily tuning their instruments and the atmosphere was warm and friendly, just the thing on a November evening. The Duck interior was on two levels – the restaurant was on the raised area separated by a sort of balustrade that gave the diners a bird's eye view of the group. In the lower part of the room there were tables and chairs and two corner booths with inset tables. By the end of the night there seemed to be people jammed in everywhere. There was bound to be some health and safety rule somewhere about the number of occupants a room should have. However, it had never been adhered to.

The group were more or less set up when Angus dashed in, apologising for being late.

"Hi, Liz, sorry, mother had run out of her painkillers and I had to run to McLeish's. She insists you got her some the other day but they were definitely not in the cupboard where she keeps them. Never mind, I'm here now. Won't keep you a minute. I'll just catch my breath."

"Actually, Angus, I did get Iona's tablets from McLeish the day I was there decorating her bedroom. She told me you had already got them, but we couldn't find them either. That's strange."

"Oh God, don't tell me she is going senile?"

"No, never, your mum is as bright as a button. No, there has to be another explanation."

The room had begun to fill. Usually the group began playing as people came in – it made for a nicer atmosphere.

They went into a few fast reels to get the night off to a good start, with locals shouting out requests of the type that everyone would sing to.

"In a neat little town they call Belfast… Her eyes they shone like diamonds… And her hair hung over her shoulder, tied up with a black velvet band…"

'The March of the Hens' was a favourite and was usually when Angus would lift Liz up on to a chair or a table. This was a tune that sounded like hens marching, so the music was, of course, the fiddle chhh, chhh, chhh… The tune became faster as the fiddle played rapidly and Liz's feet tapped almost as quickly as the bow on her fiddle.

They played another sing-along favourite, 'The Four Poster Bed', and as the night flew on it was soon time to stop for a drink before the last songs, which usually became quite rowdy. While sitting drinking a tall glass of thirst-quenching tonic water, Liz had a chance to see who had just sat down on the upper level and were obviously having a meal together – Fiona and Ben.

Break over, Liz hadn't any time to dwell on the fact that Fiona was here in Juniper Green and not in Edinburgh, which begged the question: was she staying overnight or driving back this evening?

The group performed some mournful songs from Irish folk history, which Angus played beautifully on the Irish flute, sending shivers down any music lover's spine. Liz tried not to let her gaze slide over towards Ben and

Fiona's table, as Fiona seemed to be in deep discussion and quite clearly not interested in the music at all. Yet quite often Liz could see Ben tapping his feet under the table.

As the night came almost to a close, the group played their signature song, which usually brought the house down. It was impossible to have a normal conversation during it, and frustration could quite clearly be seen on Fiona's face as she attempted to put her hands over her ears in an effort to deaden the noise. However, Ben, it would seem, wanted to join in this song as the whole place erupted in tune:

I've been a wild rover for many a year,
And I spent all my money on whiskey and beer.
And now I'm returning with gold in great store,
And I never will play the wild rover no more.

Chorus: And it's no, nay, never,

No, nay, never no more,
Will I play the wild rover,
No, never, no more.

I went to an ale-house I used to frequent,
And told the landlady my money was spent.
I asked her for credit, she answered me,
"Nay,
Such custom as yours I could have any
day."

Chorus:

I took from my pocket ten sovereigns bright,
And the landlady's eyes opened wide with
delight.
She said, "I have whiskey and wines of the
best,
And the words that I spoke, sure, were only
in jest."

Chorus:

I'll go home to my parents, confess what I've done,
And I'll ask them to pardon their prodigal son.
And if they caress me as all times before,
Sure I never will play the wild rover no more.

Each time the chorus came round the whole room would erupt into table banging, floor stamping and hand clapping. It was irresistible – even those few individuals who had never heard this particular tune before could not resist the clap of the hand or the stamp of the foot. And quite clearly Ben could not resist the stamping of his feet and the slap of his hands on to his thighs, at which Fiona was absolutely astounded. Not to mention being increasingly annoyed at the interruption to whatever the important conversation she was attempting to have with Ben was about.

As they repeated the last chorus once again, and everyone sang at the tops of their voices, it brought the whole pub to an explosive climax, to shouts and whistles and calls for “More, more.”

This, thought Liz, was what music was all about – the pleasure, the sheer thrill, the excitement knowing that a few musicians could bring such joy to so many people, and uplift them as they wended their weary ways home, humming a tune.

As everyone began to leave the pub and the group started to pack away their instruments, Liz was acutely aware of Ben and Fiona filing past. Liz heard Fiona say quite clearly, “This is not what I expected when you suggested a meal out, Ben.” She heard Ben’s reply even more clearly: “Oh, wasn’t it? It was even better than I’d expected, actually.”

Liz gave a wry, secret smile and carried on packing as Ben gave a distant nod in her direction when they left the building.

Chapter 15

On Wednesday morning, bright and early, Liz was working at the Mill, decorating the lounge for Mrs Burns, or Hannah, as she insisted Liz call her. Later that afternoon she couldn't help overhearing a rather heated discussion between Hannah and her daughter. Apparently Hannah had run out of her arthritis medication and would need it before Isla, her daughter, went home. Isla had called in to help put her mother's furniture back into place and re-hang her curtains after the decoration was finished. She hadn't really wanted to go to McLeish's for medication, which she was sure she had got a few days previously, anyway.

However, it was obvious that the tablets were nowhere to be seen, so while Isla nipped to McLeish's Liz began to collect all her dust sheets and stuff, piling them at the door and pushing furniture back into place as she went. When the door opened and in walked Mrs Monroe, the scheme manager, or warden, as she preferred to be called. Liz was a little taken back as she hadn't heard her knock.

"Oh, Mrs Cassidy… I didn't know you were here, I didn't see your van outside?"

"No, well, I parked around by the back door – it's closer to Hannah's flat. Less distance to carry all my stuff, as you can see. It's amazing how much stuff you need to do one job."

Liz indicated her pile of sheets et cetera piled against the wall. Mrs Monroe looked a little taken aback, saying, "I, er… Just called to see how Hannah is, erm, she's getting worse, you know…"

"Oh, her arthritis, you mean? Yes, I know. Isla has just gone to McLeish's to get her some more tablets. She'll be back in a minute if you wanted to see her?"

"No, no, er… I'll catch her another time. I just thought I'd call to make sure she is all righ. She's becoming very forgetful, but if you and her daughter are here then that's fine."

As Mrs Monroe left, Hannah came through from the kitchen where she had been putting some money into an envelope to give to Liz. Liz knew that it would consist of the amount she had quoted, plus a substantial tip, which she dare not refuse or Hannah would be very hurt.

"Was that the door? Is Isla back?"

"No, no, it was Mrs Monroe; she called to see if you were all right, but said she would call again later."

"Oh… All right. I know she's kind and she does come and check on me quite a lot, but I wish she wouldn't just walk in with her key; she sometimes give me a terrible fright. Especially if I'm in bed late at night or early in the morning. Oh, I know I should be grateful, and I'm not saying I'm not, it's just a little… Well…

"Thank you, my dear, you've made a beautiful job of the lounge and even pushed the furniture back. You have no idea how it feels to have my little flat all clean for Christmas. You probably think I'm an old fool but it means a lot to me. I used to have a lovely little cottage, and don't get me wrong, I love my little flat, but I just wish I had the energy and the strength to do the things I used to… Old age, you know, it creeps up on you before you're ready."

After saying her goodbyes, Liz decided she would take Barnie out for his walk and on the way back she would treat herself to fish and chips from the village chippy.

Not something she did everyday but she had worked hard today and couldn't wait to have something to eat and a nice hot bath. After having her fish supper and her lovely hot bath Liz was all dressed in her warm winter red dressing gown in front of the log burner when she decided to return her mum's call from Tuesday evening and see if she seemed any happier.

Florence Saint was a very smart, very svelte good-looking woman in her late sixties. She had retired and moved to Benidorm for the sunshine. She hated the winters in England, she would say. But the truth was that she and her companions, most of whom were of the male variety, simply enjoyed lazing around in the sun all day, topping up their tans and drinking margaritas. Liz often told her mum it sounded more like wrinklies lying around baking like sardines in the sun while waiting for God. Liz knew her mother was an organiser, a doer, yet there she was seemingly wasting her life. It seemed such a shame, but who was Liz to interfere?

She wondered how her mother had got over the shock of Byron and Terry going. Maybe that would be a little too close to the waiting for God bit and she might change her mind and come home; even though Liz knew that if her mother were in England they would argue like cat and dog. Her mum felt it was her duty to find a new husband for Liz. She truly thought that no woman should be without a man – or, in her case, several.

"How are you, Mum? Have you got over the shock yet about Byron and Terry?"

"Oh, Liz, things aren't the same any more. When I look over to Byron's condo, I can't help but miss him – and Terry, of course. Things are changing all the time… But never mind me – how are you? Have you met any nice men yet? You know, Bob wouldn't have wanted you to remain single all your life. You're still young. You're not still doing that decorating work, are you? You'll never meet a nice man if you're buried under dust sheets and dungarees all day."

How ironic that was, thought Liz. Fact could be stranger than fiction, or something like that, if she only knew.

"Mum, Mum, I like my work and I do meet people – I meet them when I'm at the Duck – and I know Bob wouldn't mind. You sound like Tom – he thinks I should go out more and meet someone… As long as it's not Nigel."

"Well, I'm not surprised Tom wouldn't want you to stay with Niiigel – he's a pain, and he uses you Liz. You're the only one that can't see it. Anyway, didn't you say something the other night about not seeing him as much any more in the future? What's that all about? What's happening? Is there some gossip? Has he met a woman and decided she's better than you?"

"God, you're as bad as Isabel! No, he hasn't found another woman… Although I suppose he has, in a manner of speaking. Well, you know the house I've been working on… Juniper Manor. You know, the architect who has moved into the village from Edinburgh? Well, wait for it – he has offered to do all the plans for the new village hall for free! Nigel nearly fell off the stage when Ben announced his goodwill gesture at the meeting… And…"

"Ben? Ben, is that his name? You're on first name terms, then?"

"God, talk about the Spanish inquisition – you are wasted, you know that? Yes, Ben is his name, and yes, I'm on first name terms. After all, I decorated his whole house for him."

"Is he nice-looking? Tell me what he looks like. Is he tall and dark? Oh, don't tell me, he looks like Niiigel. Please don't tell me that. He's not married, is he? Or old? How old? Is he old?"

"Jesus, let me get a word in, Mum, and I'll tell you the gen, for goodness sake. Yes, he is nice, he is, erm, good-looking in a Hugh Grant sort of way, and he looks to be about late thirties, early forties, so no, he is not in his dotage. Meanwhile, back at the story I was going to tell you about Nigel and Ben's partner Fiona…"

"He has a partner? You never mentioned her before. Are they engaged? Do they live together? What's she like?"

"Mum, I said partner as in work partner! I don't think they are partners as in a couple. Well, I don't think so, put it that way. And meanwhile, back at the ranch, Nigel seems to be rather taken with the fact that she is not only an architect, but she is also very pretty and business orientated. He is very, very impressed, and has suddenly got his important hat on. He has it in his mind that he personally is going to build the new village hall with the help of Ben and Fiona."

"Oh, that's wonderful news. That means he'll be too busy to have you running all over, especially if there's a woman involved. Oh, Liz, you will have to make it your business to find out if this Fiona woman is 'handsome Ben's' bed partner as well as his work partner."

"Oh, Mum, for goodness sake, how on earth am I supposed to do that? Even supposing I want to…"

Liz was asking herself the same question – how would she know? She still didn't know if Fiona had stopped with Ben last night. It would have been too late to travel back to Edinburgh, surely. Although she would have to have been back in the office this morning, Liz reasoned. Oh, she thought, her mum always did this to her – got her mind working on something she knew she wanted to know but was trying to pretend to herself that she wasn't the slightest bit interested in.

"What does Isabel think of this Ben person? Does she think he's handsome? Ha ha, I bet she's pleased as punch about Niiigel being busy with larger fish to fry. Be careful, though, you're not out of the woods yet. Who has he roped in to do the panto?"

"Mum, you're as bad as Isabel! I've done my part. Well, I've done the scenery, and I have still got to find some material and make some shepherds' costumes and odds and sods, but that's all, and I don't mind doing that. After all, it is for the village. The thing is he won't need me for anything to do with the new hall – he doesn't class me as able enough to do any of the paperwork, unlike Fiona, and although I am a decorator he won't need me for that until the hall is built."

“And, my girl, he wouldn’t want you to get any of the glory. Do you think this Fiona would be interested in Niiigel?”

“Oh, I don’t think so, Mum, she is a top architect from Edinburgh, and I think her sights are set on Ben if she hasn’t already got him hooked. Listen to me, between you and Isabel you’ve got me as bad as yourselves. More to the point, Mum, are you okay? Are you still happy over there? Are you sure you don’t want to come back?”

“Oh, I’m fine. I’m sure things will get better once someone moves into Byron’s condo, although I really hope Frank and Mable change their mind and stay. Don’t you worry about me, I’m having a ball.

“Listen, you better go, dear, this phone call will be costing you a fortune, and, anyway, I’m off out for drinkies at one of the newbies’ villa down the road. Bye for now, darling,” Florence said in a theatrical voice, wishing her daughter adieu, and off she went.

Part of Liz would love her mum to come back to England, but the other part knew that as long as she was miles away she couldn't embarrass her by inviting every single male within miles to her so-called drinks evenings, which Liz simply had to attend.

Liz met Isabel the following morning in the village's only little coffee shop. It was warm and cosy and all the beautiful cakes were home-made by locals as a village venture to help with funding for one good cause or another. The temptation was much harder for Isabel, as she had what used to be called a voluptuous figure, which required her to keep a tight rein on her calorie intake.

Liz, on the other hand, could eat until the cows came home and never put on an ounce. In fact, if it wasn't for her very womanly bust, it would be hard to tell when she had her dungarees on if she was a woman or a man. Especially if she had her baseball cap on, which she always wore while painting ceilings to keep the spots off her hair.

"Well, I'm having a piece of cheesecake. To hell with my calorie counting for today. You, no doubt, will have a huge piece of carrot cake and not gain an ounce?"

"Yes, sorry, but I think I burned even more off yesterday painting Hannah Burns' lounge. Listen, are we still on for Saturday? I must make a definite start with my Christmas shopping."

"Yes, definitely. What's it like not being pestered by Niiigel? Or has he been in touch? I bet he has – he won't be able to function without you to think for him."

"Actually no, I haven't heard a word from him, and I feel a little guilty because I've actually had a wonderful week. I even took the day off on Tuesday, which meant I was at my best for the group. It was a good night, wasn't it?"

Liz knew exactly what she was doing; she was drawing Isabel in so that she could ask about Ben and Fiona. And, sure enough, Isabel fell for it hook, line and sinker.

"Well, Ben seemed to enjoy the performance; I could see his feet tapping away from where I was sitting. Don't tell me you didn't see them? I don't think Fiona liked it, though – she looked very serious and quite obviously didn't know it was to be a live music night."

"Well, how strange, because I told Ben we would be playing if he felt like calling in, as I told you. Anyway, you and Angus seemed to be having a close tête-à-tête during the interval. What gives?"

"Nothing; I just think he's a nice guy, that's all, and he's single. There's nothing in it, mind. We are just friends, so leave it at that, nosey."

"Me nosey? Good grief, you are the queen of nosey! Me? Ha, now there's a thing. So you'll be coming tomorrow night as usual, hmmm?"

They laughed together as they both knew that it wasn't Liz who was the nosey one; she was just doing what Isabel normally did when there was any hint of romance or scandal in the air. They parted still laughing and agreed to meet at the Duck tomorrow evening as usual.

Chapter 16

To Liz's utter surprise, when she and Isabel arrived at the Duck the following evening, roughly fifteen minutes before starting time, who should be sitting at the table close to where the musicians took their rest in the interval but the man himself, looking super casual in a black shirt and black trousers. He looks rather nice, thought Liz, just as Isabel gave her the shove of an elbow to indicate those very thoughts.

He immediately jumped up to help her with her two instrument cases, as they appeared huge in comparison to Liz herself. One, of course, was her fiddle and the other her bodhrán, or Irish drum, which was used in the jigs and the reels as they were usually pretty fast. They were the tunes that encouraged any normal music lover to stamp their feet or clap their hands.

“Hello. You’re either a glutton for punishment or you really enjoyed it the other night?”

Ben said hello to Isabel and Liz, telling them that he had enjoyed himself so much but had felt restricted as it had been supposed to be a business meeting the other evening. So tonight he was going to enjoy every moment of it.

“Well, I’m glad you liked it. I suppose I should have warned you – it can get very, very rowdy, and it’s not exactly the place to have a quiet meal.”

“With your girlfriend,” Isabel chirped in, with the intention of sifting for information.

Ben was wise, but not bad-mannered, and he also realised there was no malice in Isabel, just a natural curiosity, so he played along a little, saying, “Oh, I’ll know the next time… Actually, I had forgotten I had arranged a business meeting with my partner, but at the same time I really wanted to come and hear the group play, so I have to own up and say

I neglected to tell Fiona about the live music. She wasn't best pleased as she isn't a music fan of any description. Actually, I'm not quite sure, apart from work, what she is a fan of. I, on the other hand, loved every moment of it and cannot honestly say I heard a word she said all evening. However, I do think I agreed to whatever it was."

"Ohhwa, that could be dangerous," said Isabel. "I hope you enjoy it tonight, Ben. I'll catch ya later – I want to have a drink with Angus before you start, Liz."

"Yes, yes, okay, Isabel, see you later."

Isabel gave Liz an outrageous wink, which she was positive Ben couldn't have failed to see, quite obviously allowing Liz and Ben time with each other before the group got going. Liz's face had gone bright red at Isabel's blatant attempt at matchmaking. She decided the only way to tackle it was head on, so that Ben wouldn't feel like a victim.

"I'm sorry about Isabel… And her blatant matchmaking. I'm afraid, because I'm a, er, widow, I have become fair game for all my well-meaning family and friends to assist me back into matrimony. Please feel free to run now, but be assured I take absolutely no notice of any of them, so you are perfectly safe from me. My only weapons are my fiddle and my dog, of course, but tonight I hope you really enjoy the fiddle."

"I can hardly wait. Actually, as a boy I played the drums a little. Not very well, but with great enthusiasm, much to my poor parents' horror, especially as they didn't buy them for me. I swapped with another boy for a very expensive guitar that they *did* buy for me, but that was far too difficult to learn quickly. And as I wanted to be a rock star immediately, the drums seemed the fastest way to reach my goal."

"Ha, and in the end you became an architect and left all the music behind? So, can you keep a beat?"

"Oh, well, yes, he says modestly, I think so."

As Liz opened one of her instrument cases and took out her bodhrán, she explained that basically all you had to do when playing the Irish drum was to keep the beat. And she gave Ben a quick and simple demonstration.

"For example, I'll tell you if it's a jig or a reel, and the simplest beat for each is either down, down, up, down, up; or *one*, two, three, four, five, six, seven, eight – with the emphasis on the one. And that's it! Simple as that for the tunes we will be playing tonight. If you would like to join in, have a little practice. Don't feel pressured, though. If you don't want to join in then just sit and listen, but you are very welcome to try."

Liz showed Ben how to hold the stick, which simply beat the drum, and showed him where to place his hand inside the drum to deaden the noise. Ben was like an excited child – he could hardly wait and seemed game for anything.

The group began tuning up and Angus detached himself from Isabel, rather slowly, thought Liz with great delight. She would like to see Isabel with someone permanent like Angus, who was the sweetest man but would never be described as such, being so huge. And Isabel was the kindest of people, who had been so unlucky in her own love life. It would be nice if they found happiness together.

The group began to play, and tonight it was Angus who took the lead on his flute as he played ‘Molly Malone’ to get the locals in the singing mood. Everyone knew such a famous tune. The haunting sounds of the flute were softly played and again it was hard to reconcile Angus with having such a delicate touch. That tune rolled into ‘Biddy Mulligan’, which was a livelier tune. Then came ‘Fiddler’s Green’, before they stopped for a little break before the rowdy songs began. By then most of the diners had at least had a chance to eat before the jumping up and down started.

“How are you managing?” Liz said to an exhilarated Ben, though she need hardly have asked as he looked so happy to be part of the whole ambience of the evening.

“I’m absolutely enjoying every moment, but I hope my duff notes are not spoiling any of the songs?”

“No, no, you’re doing terrifically well, and, honestly, the whole idea is that everyone is so busy singing that no one cares if there are a few missed notes. The thing is to enjoy what you are doing. I know at the beginning you are so busy counting that you can’t enjoy it like the audience do, but you soon get better and better, and find you’re doing it without thinking.”

“I am so excited. This is my rock star moment twenty years too late.”

“If you find you simply want to stop playing and sing then just sing. At the beginning of the night, sometimes the audience are a little timid, but by the end of the night you can’t keep them down and that's when the whole night becomes so exciting.

"Bob used to play a lot of blue grass on the banjo and he could have the place jumping in no time. And Tom, when he is home, he plays the whistle. He is brilliant! He'll be home at Christmas so you must come then and meet him."

"I'd like that," Ben said with feeling and a look in his eyes that promised he would be there. When the break was over and everyone's thirst quenched, they began the second part with a song called 'Seven Drunken Nights', which promised whole audience participation and never failed to lift the roof. This was a good one for Ben to hit the bodhrán in without needing to worry if he was out of tune; it was unlikely anyone would notice. After a couple of short reels and a jig it was announced that the song before 'The Wild Rover' would be 'Three Lovely Lassies from Kimmage'. This tune was an absolute favourite with everybody joining in; and, on Liz's advice, Ben laid down his drum so that he could enjoy the atmosphere of the whole crowd in the pub.

The first verse began thus:

There were three lovely lasses from Kimmage,
From Kimmage, from Kimmage, from Kimmage
And whenever there was a bit of a scrimmage
Sure I was the toughest of all
Sure I was the toughest of all.

Well, it was obvious from the first that the whole audience would repeat the chorus every time, becoming more and more rowdy as the verses went on. It told the story of one of the lovely lasses getting the prize of the 'man'; then went on to tell of her mounting number of children and continuing search for accommodation, though, in the meantime, she would live with [said in a broad Irish accent] "me ma; in the meantime we'll live with me ma."

It ended with screams of delight, Ben cheering and whistling, along with everyone else, to the group to play more, which of course they always did. At least one more chorus.

As the night flew by it was time to play their signature tune, 'The Wild Rover', and once again the stamping and clapping could be heard outside in the car park, which signalled that a great night was being had by all. Liz looked over to where Ben was sitting and she smiled at the sight of him, all flushed with sheer excitement and with pleasure written all over him. She wondered what his work colleagues in Edinburgh would make of the workaholic tonight.

"You look as though you've enjoyed yourself tonight?"

"Do you know, I can't remember when I last had more enjoyment than I've had tonight? Honestly I can't. I've had a wonderful time.

I can see why you love your Tuesdays and Thursdays so much. The group are wonderful and the audience just love you all and they know all the songs and all the verses, don't they? How on earth?"

"Ha ha, well, most of them come on and off every week or so, so they know roughly what we'll play. We like to mix it up a little, though. We used to have Bob on the banjo, which was wonderful, and Angus, of course. He is amazing, isn't he? Can you believe such a soft haunting sound comes out of such a big man? Tony, of course, can play any stringed instrument, but obviously not at the same time, so it depends on the tunes as to what he plays. Oh, the mandolin is wonderful, isn't it? And Kevin plays the banjo brilliantly, of course. He is almost as good as Bob was…"

Ben could see that talking about Bob brought back piquant memories, happy and sad ones, so he did his best to change the conversation to a lighter topic.

"So, hey, you can't possibly go straight home to bed after this excitement, surely?"

"No, I can never sleep straight after a gig so I usually take Barnie out for a run then home for a hot drink before bed."

"That sounds wonderful. I wonder if you would mind a little company this evening, or do you like to be alone?"

Liz was actually taken aback and suddenly thought to herself, did she mind? Well, actually, no, she didn't. In fact, she would enjoy the company.

"Er, no, no, you're more than welcome to come, though it's nothing exciting – the whole idea is that I wind down… Of course… But yes, please come, that would be nice."

As the group packed all their instruments away and began to leave the Duck, Liz saw Isabel and Angus wandering out together, Isabel mouthing that she would give her a ring tomorrow. So Liz decided to get her own back by giving an exaggerated wink as they left the pub, Isabel pretending not to notice.

Ben followed Liz's little van back to her cottage and parked directly behind. Liz had visions of Mrs Mangle's face being pressed against the window in the dark to see if she recognised the car. She certainly wouldn't be able to, though, because Liz realised that she hadn't even seen Ben's car in daylight before. He was driving a brand new Range Rover, although somehow she had imagined at first that he would have a BMW.

Ben carried Liz's instruments into the passage and followed her into the warm cosy kitchen, where Barnie had been lying in front of the Aga in his giant bed. When he saw Liz wasn't alone Barnie recognised Ben immediately and pushed his long face into Ben's hand in greeting. He couldn't believe his luck when Liz got his lead from the hook on the wall and it became obvious that he was going out with both of them.

Barnie was the most calm and unexcitable animal, usually. The most excited he became was when he gave a rhythmic swish of his tail, which was just as well, as some dogs have a tendency to jump up. If Barnie had done that he would have knocked a person flying, or flattened them altogether.

As Ben and Liz walked around the common, Liz with her torch and Ben throwing a ball into the pitch black of the night, it was amazing that Barnie found it within minutes and was back to start over again. Ben, being an architect, was often on building sites, so always had a warm coat and wellingtons in the boot of his car, which meant that he was suitably dressed for dog walking.

"You have a wonderful life, don't you, Liz? There's no pressure. I mean, you know how to enjoy your life. I don't mean you haven't had tragedy in your life, I realise you have, but you seem to have adjusted and you have a wonderful network of friends and colleagues who have similar interests."

"Well, I have a good life, I agree, though it wasn't so good when Bob died or when he was ill. But yes, I do have a wonderful network of friends who have helped me to cope. If it hadn't been for the group, and Isabel and Tom, of course, I'm not sure how I would have coped. But I love my music and could never see the day when I wasn't part of the band. They all knew Bob as well, so they feel they need to protect me and I feel safe with them. Isabel is my best friend from school days so we know each other inside and out. And I actually love my work. It's not always as challenging as I would like and I would really love to do something more worthwhile artistically, if you know what I mean, but, on the whole, I'm very, very lucky and happier than I've been for a long time."

This last sentiment was said while glancing across at Ben's profile in the dark. And to Liz's surprise she actually meant it. Suddenly she realised she was really happy for the first time in such a long time and didn't feel guilty about it. She knew that she was glad that Ben had moved into the village and knew also that she liked bumping into him or there being the possibility that she may bump into him in a shop or on the common or in the Duck. So yes, she was happier, she thought to herself.

Ben started hesitantly but eventually began to tell Liz about his practice in Edinburgh and how he had built it up from scratch, how it was a very well-known and very well-respected company in the city. When he had begun to attract more business than he could possibly handle, he'd taken Fiona on as a partner, as she was already a successful architect herself with a small practice of her own, also in Edinburgh. They had never looked back since, although they had in some ways become victims of their own success, meaning that their lives had become non-existent and their work had become all. Fiona didn't seem to mind this, it seemed, Ben told Liz even more hesitantly as though there was something he couldn't bring himself to say. But it hadn't gone that way for him.

“Eventually,” he said, “I became ill and was advised to change my lifestyle for my own good. I got such a fright. Then I decided that only I could change my lifestyle and that the only way to do that would be to leave the city. Don’t get me wrong, I love the city, I get a buzz from it, but it’s like a drug to me. I can’t seem to stop once I’m there. Coming to this village is the best and the most outrageous thing I’ve ever done for myself, since setting up my own business when I had only just left university.

“I have never actually enjoyed myself so much in a very, very long time. I’d almost forgotten how to. I had begun to think that basically there was only work, which actually used to give me such a lot of pleasure. But then I realised that I was doing a lot of work that I didn’t enjoy just because it was what the client wanted, or was very well paid. Then, after my health scare, I decided to change my lifestyle and my choice of work. I don’t mean being an architect – I still love that work – but I only want to work on buildings or projects that I find challenging. You know. As you say, there is bread and butter work, but to find something that gives you self-satisfaction, is something worth doing… Well, I think, anyway…

"Listen to me rabbitting on! You're supposed to be relaxing after a wonderful night. Which is what I started to say and got lost. I've had a wonderful evening and I really hope you will allow me to join in again?"

"You have not been rabbitting on, and I'm so pleased you had a wonderful night. Of course you are more than welcome any time. Really, I mean that."

Arriving back at the cottage Liz was positive that she saw Mrs Mangle's curtains twitching and was almost tempted to put her arm around Ben just to give her something to see. The very thought made her laugh out loud, leading Ben to enquire, "What? What is it?"

He smiled at her, realising that something had tickled her fancy.

“I just had a naughty thought. You must forgive me, but you haven’t lived in a village long enough to see every little twitch of the curtain yet. So you have no idea that at this very moment you have an audience – and sometimes, out of pure devilment, I feel like playing up to it.”

“Who is watching? Tell me!”

He was beginning to turn, smiling and looking, when Liz pulled at his sleeve saying, “No, no, don’t turn around, she’ll see you.”

As they neared the front door and were safely out of sight, Liz and Ben were consumed with the giggles. Liz explained about Mrs Mangle.

“She sees everything and, to be honest, most of the time it makes me feel very safe and secure knowing that no one could ever break in or attack me without her spotting something was wrong. However, it would be impossible to carry on a clandestine relationship without her knowing what time he arrived and left."

They laughed together, flopping down into a chair after a fit of the giggles, realising that two grown people were afraid of a nosey neighbour.

"And have you?"

"What?"

"Had a clandestine relationship?"

"No, ha ha, no, I have not," Liz said, a little outraged but knowing it was all in fun.

"So you and Nigel were never…?"

"No, we were not! Although that's a bit harsh on Nigel; he would have liked us to be. But I never wanted Nigel in that way. To be honest, I feel a bit guilty about Nigel. He seemed to fill a void after Bob died. He was always there, you know? But then I suddenly began to realise that I didn't really want to be in a relationship with him and I could see that he was becoming impatient, and a little bit of a control freak. If the village hall project hadn't regenerated just at the right time I think I would have had to bite the bullet and tell him. Whereas this way he thinks that he has let me down gently, as he hasn't got time for me and that suits us both."

They gravitated towards the lovely warm kitchen and Barnie flopped down into his bed and within seconds was fast asleep.

"Wow, he really is the perfect pet – company one minute then asleep the next."

They sat at the table with their hot chocolate, chatting amiably about the night's entertainment, and Ben confided in Liz that the more he lived in the village the less he wanted to go back to the city.

"You know, at one time I lived for the buzz of the city, the bright lights, the sounds, sirens flashing past every few minutes. The city at lighting up time in the early evening was when I came to life. I could have worked all day and on into the early hours or on to a club for a drink late into the night.

"But, for some reason, it all seems so far away now and unimportant. I wonder when I became obsessed with work and forgot to enjoy my life. I sound a little like Scrooge, but, you know, at first I simply wanted to get my practice started. Then you want to secure your future, financially, for the time when you get married and have a family. Then, before you realise it, you haven't had time to get married or have a family and it's almost too late…" Ben seemed to stop in mid sentence as though there was more that he couldn't say.

"Now I've made the move and I love it, I wonder why it took me so long to see it. I really did enjoy myself tonight and I owe it all to you."

"Don't be silly, you don't owe me anything, but I'm so glad you have enjoyed yourself. When Bob died I needed the music. I felt safe with the band and they understood how I felt. And they are a great bunch. You'll find once you are involved in the village you will soon have lots of friends. Just be very careful what you say."

"Why?" Ben said quizzically.

"Because, Ben Paris, you are a villager's dream… Fresh meat, fresh news, and within two minutes of your invitation to 'call in any time', they will, and you will never get any work done at home. People never understand about working from home – they think you are basically 'at home' – so just remember, the village is watching and listening."

Liz and Ben laughed companionably together before Liz said she was going to chuck him out into the night before Mrs Mangle thought she had a strange man in the house. "God knows what she thought the night you stayed over. It hasn't filtered back to me yet, which is strange."

They walked towards the front door, where Ben pulled on his jacket and boots. As he straightened up he caught hold of one of Liz's hands, gently drawing her towards him. Liz lifted her eyes in surprise and, as she did, he leant forward and kissed her gently on the cheek.

"Thank you, Lizy, I've enjoyed our time together."

And with that he was gone, out of the door and into his car and away.

Chapter 17

After a restless night's sleep where Liz continually relived the surprising encounter at the door with Ben, Liz decided she couldn't sleep any longer and got up, determined to go into town to finish collecting materials for the panto.

After trawling through the charity shops Liz was very happy with her collection of usable items. Once home she began to sew the different materials into various shepherds' costumes for the children's nativity. And she proceeded to make the wedding dress and two bridesmaids' dresses she had picked up at an obscene price into ball gowns for the *Cinderella* show. Very happy with her morning's work and feeling her work was complete on the village pantomime, Liz decided to drop the costumes off at the village hall where there was always some activity go on.

She came across a very odd situation, as she was unpacking the suit bags where she had carefully laid the ball gowns. She knew she couldn't carry everything and decided she would have to come back for the shepherds' costumes so she left the doors of the van open. But just as she was rooting around in the van with the doors obscuring her from view, something caught her eye. Just outside the old Mill's back door she could see Mrs Monroe and a young man engrossed in some sort of argument.

The young man appeared to have a hold of Mrs Monroe's wrist and was twisting it. She was just about to intervene when Mrs Monroe smiled and seemed to reassure the young man, saying something that appeared to appease him, and he walked away without a backward glance. Then Mrs Monroe looked around rather furtively, in Liz's view, then went quickly back inside.

Liz dropped the costumes behind the stage, leaving a note for Celia, and hoped that was the last she would hear about the pantomime until she was sitting watching it in the audience.

The following morning Liz met Isabel bright and early, so they could spend the whole day in town together as they had when they were young. They both had lists of Christmas presents they wanted, so Isabel parked in the large car park in the centre of town to enable them to keep popping back with their goodies.

After three hours of shopping they eventually stopped for lunch and to give their feet a rest, as Isabel had unwisely worn heeled shoes as opposed to Liz's comfortable tucker boots. As they sat in the little café idly chatting, a group of teenagers in the corner appeared to be doing something very furtive, which reminded Liz about the previous day's encounter.

"Tell me if you think I'm just being paranoid but…" Liz retold the story about the teenager and Mrs Monroe, and waited for Isabel's reaction.

“How odd. Although I don’t trust him, it sounds like her son, you know the one? He lives on the new council estate. I’ve heard he is a nasty piece of work and into drugs and all sorts.”

“Oh, you mean the estate they’ve just built on the edge of town?”

“Yes, they say he lives with a girl from the town in a flat, apparently, although I can’t say for sure. They do say he is a bad lot, though.”

The conversation was instantly forgotten as they carried on with their lunch. They then decided they had as many presents as they needed, having been back to Isabel’s car twice.

Isabel declared, “It’s time to buy us some Christmas glitter.”

The strange thing was that two weeks ago, if Isabel had suggested Liz buy anything to wear, she would have laughed it off and poo-pooed it. However, Liz decided it wouldn't do any harm to have possibly a little black number, just in case she needed one. And maybe even a new skirt and top or shoes – she could afford it, so why not?

They had great fun. It was like old times when they were teenagers and used to choose clothes together, only this time they actually had the money to buy the clothes instead of just trying them on then leaving the shop saying they didn't actually like anything, and giggling all the way home.

Isabel held up a lovely little black number encouraging Liz to give it a try as it was her size and she would really suit it. Then when Liz came out of the changing room, Isabel whistled saying it really, really suited her. The dress was a simple style in an extra fine merino wool. It had a scoop neckline and it fitted like a sleeve before flaring slightly below the waistline into tiny little pleats that swished as Liz paraded along the corridor in order to show it off to Isabel. This dress would only suit a figure like Liz's, whose shape was not unlike that of a slim boy but with curves in the right places, as Isabel would say enviously.

"You must buy that or I will be furious as well as annoyingly envious that I cannot wear such a dress. You look gorgeous, Liz, really, you must buy it."

Isabel was so in earnest about her buying the dress that Liz felt she had no option, although when she would wear such a dress was beyond her. Isabel bought a plum-coloured dress of soft jersey that also flared but more or less from the waist and suited her figure extremely well. Isabel insisted that while she had Liz's attention she must buy herself some smart casuals.

"I'm sure you haven't been shopping since Bob died and you are not being disloyal simply looking smart. Tom would agree and now that I don't have to worry about you dressing yourself up for Niiigel I would like you to look glam again like you used to."

"Well, thank you, that makes me sound as though I have been looking like a bag lady."

"Well, I don't mean to be cruel, but you do have a tendency to wear your dungarees or jeans a lot. Even Barnie has noticed how scruffy you look compared to him."

Liz did love her trousers and jeans, but this time, for a change, she bought herself a pair of soft black cords that teamed up with a charcoal fine wool polo neck sweater and the mannequin model was also wearing a knitted biker jacket that suited Liz to perfection. Isabel, on the other hand, who didn't particularly wear a lot of trousers, went for a heavy jersey shift dress in bright red with a crop edge to edge jacket in the same material in black.

Isabel, having Liz's undivided attention for once, began to whiz through various clothing racks, in order to tempt Liz into buying more. But Liz began to leave the department thinking they had at last exhausted their stock. Until all of a sudden Isabel's eye caught on a gorgeous tweed duffle jacket, in deep green, with a navy, blue and red stripe. This she knew would not suit her but would look fantastic on Liz.

She dragged her back from the exit, telling her she must try it on, and her hunch paid off as Liz looked terrific in it.

"Oh, Liz, it's a House of Bruar, and it's pure wool, and you look lovely in it, and it's reduced – what more can you want? Please buy it. You won't regret it, it's one of those little jackets that you'll never regret, honestly."

"Oh, I don't know, do I need it? Will I wear it? Even reduced, can I warrant spending that much on a jacket?" Liz was saying, all the while twirling back and forth, trying to see the pleat in the centre of the jacket that fell just on to her bottom and fitted like a dream. Even the lining felt luxurious.

"Oh, go on, Liz, you look classy in it and it will go with those lovely cords you've just bought."

"Oh, go on then. I am never coming shopping with you again, you tempt me too much. Although it's nice, isn't it, that here we are all these years later and we can actually afford to buy these lovely things instead of just trying them on? Yes, I will have it. Why not?"

"That a girl! Now we can go to the car, I'm exhausted. Making you buy clothes is a very tiring business."

"Me too. Let me buy us a takeaway and we'll go back to my house. Why don't you stay over and we can have a couple of bottles of wine. We should push the boat out today – it's been a Nigel free day, have you noticed? Thank God for the village and the importance of being Nigel."

Chapter 18

On Sunday morning Liz was up early as usual. However, Isabel was still fast asleep in the spare room when Liz left to take Barnie for a walk on the common. They had demolished two bottles of white wine and an Indian takeaway while watching an ancient version of *Rebecca* on the television before falling into an exhausted sleep.

Isabel simply didn't have the stamina that Liz appeared to have; or was it that Liz knew she had to get up for poor old Barnie or face the consequences? Once out in the fresh air, Liz was always glad she had made the effort. However, this morning she wished she hadn't been quite as diligent, as the first person she met on the way to the common was Nigel. Liz's heart gave a slight sinking feeling, but she tried to sound jovial in her greeting to him.

"Hello, Nigel, fancy seeing you out so early. What brings you to the common?"

"Well, actually, I'm not, I'm on my way to the village hall but I decided to walk as my car wouldn't start. How lucky, though, that I bumped into you – I wondered how the costumes were getting on. I'm very busy now with committee business but I need to know that the panto is in good hands."

"Well now, funny you should say that, but the costumes are actually at the hall at this very moment." Liz had never been so pleased that she had decided to sew and deliver them on Friday. "They are all finished and I think you'll be very pleased with them. I left them in Celia's very capable hands the other day."

Liz let Barnie off his lead and began to walk away briskly as though it was vital that she be with Barnie. She said goodbye and that she hoped all went well with the village hall project, and she would no doubt see him on the day of the pantomime performance.

Liz rather hoped that she looked casual about her escape and that she hadn't made it look like a Benny Hill sketch.

Returning to the cottage she could smell fresh toast and coffee so it was obvious that Isabel had surfaced. When they were sat down eating their breakfast she relayed her escape.

"Guess who I met going to the common?"

"Who? Ben?"

"Nooo, what makes you think it would be Ben? No, it was Nigel."

"Oh God, no, he must have found out we were celebrating his withdrawal from the field last night."

"Ah, poor Nigel. Well, in actual fact, you would have been proud of me this morning. I made a very tactical, er, run for it after telling Nigel politely that I had finished and left all the costumes in poor Celia's capable hands. In other words, I dropped the poor woman in it, so that I could make my escape – which I did, pretending to be needed by poor old Barnie. I almost ran away! Luckily he was needed elsewhere, on important business.

"I feel pretty awful about poor Celia but, to be honest, I don't feel awful about having to do more jobs that Nigel thinks up for me. I think you're right, I need to do other things. I need to stretch myself, not just be a dog's body doing jobs that are foisted upon me."

"Well, well, who rattled your cage this morning? Good for you, my girl, you've seen the light at last."

"Don't get me wrong, I love what I do, but I feel I could do something more, although I'm not sure what, but I do know that simply filling my days with whims that Nigel dreams up is not my idea of stretching myself. Anyway, I have one or two jobs on this week then it will slow down. No one needs decorating during Christmas. Then Tom will be home for the holidays so I will enjoy spending time with him. What about you and Angus? You seem very friendly… Are you serious? Is there…romance in the air?"

"Well, to be honest, I hope so, and yes, I think he is pretty serious and actually so am I. He is a really nice guy. I don't know why we never got together sooner. I suppose I just thought of him as part of the group who I got on with. We've always joked about a lot, but lately we have talked, I mean really talked, and he has a soft generous side to him."

"I could have told you that, you idiot. He was so good to me after Bob died. He was actually my rock, not Nigel as he would have everyone believe. I also knew Angus was worried that Nigel would somehow turn my head, so to speak, but that was never going to happen. I just didn't have the energy to put up any resistance."

"And you have now? That makes me wonder… Why now? Or, rather, who now? Gives you the courage to kick Niiigel out… I have a sneaking suspicion he is an architect from Edinburgh who may also be the one to help you with that challenge you're looking for… Am I right?"

"Ha ha, don't be silly. Why on earth would Ben be interested in someone like me, a decorator from Juniper Green?"

Isabel left, tapping her nose with her finger and smiling knowingly.

Chapter 19

It was a lovely crisp winter's morning as Liz walked to the common with Barnie, who was in the middle of a mad ten minutes. It used to be a mad half hour but he was a lot older now and couldn't sustain such enthusiasm any longer. When Liz spotted the black Ranger Rover pull over towards the common, and began walking towards the figure who emerged, she knew without doubt that it was Ben. She waved in greeting as Barnie made a bee line for his new friend.

"Hi, what a lovely surprise, although I should know by now that no matter what the weather is you'll be out on the common with Barnie."

"Hi, so where are you off to this bright and early morning?"

"Well, actually, I'm on business. Listen, are you busy today?"

"No, why?"

"Would you like a trip out? I have to go and look at a castle north of Stirling. Well, I say castle – I'm expecting it to be no more than a derelict wreck. But I have been commissioned, if I decide to take it on, to renovate it. I would appreciate your company and your opinion."

"Well, yes, I would love to come and look at a castle with you, but whether my opinion would be of any use to you, I hardly think so. But yes, I would love to come. Can you give me a few minutes to take Barnie home and change?"

"Of course, but please don't dress up or anything like that. In fact, you'll need to wear your warmest and most sensible boots and things, because it could simply be a shell and I have a tendency to get very dirty and cold on these occasions, so be warned."

Liz hurried upstairs to collect a warm hat and scarf and had a sudden thought, that maybe this was the occasion to wear her new duffle jacket. It would be nice just for once for Ben to see her in something other than dog walking clothes or dungarees. She already had on her black jeans; therefore if she put her kne-length black leather boots on, the whole ensemble, she told herself, should be quite chic. Well, that was what she hoped.

"Ready when you are," Liz said, and within a few minutes they were speeding away from Juniper Green on to the bypass towards the Forth Road Bridge, going north.

"And where is this castle, do you say?"

"Well, my sat-nav is telling me it's north of Stirling, and the castle is called Muir of Orchil."

"Oh wow, sounds very interesting, and how did you find out about this job? Or do they find you? Forgive my ignorance, I don't know if your firm is really, really well known. I apologise in advance if your company is the Rolls-Royce of architectural firms, and I have never heard of you, but in my defence I have never had need of an architect's services."

"Well, we are very well known in certain circles. However, as you say, unless you are in need of an architect you wouldn't have heard of us. Within the property business we are very well known. This commission is in the balance, however – I may want to do it but Fiona certainly doesn't. She doesn't like large jobs – she says they cost more to do than they are worth and you spend a lot of time on site and quite often the clients are forever changing their original design.

"She is right, of course, but where Fiona likes to do the day-to-day or bread and butter work, as you would call it, I have become very unsatisfied with the repetition of it all and I am now ready for something that comes from the soul… If you know what I mean?

"I know that sounds pompous but it's half the reason I have detached myself almost completely from the Edinburgh practice. I know it's the kind of work that made us well known in the first place and it's where we work best and for the most profit. But, I am…"

"I know exactly what you mean, I feel exactly the same as you. Oh, don't get me wrong, I'm just a lowly decorator, but I too make a very good living from the type of work I can get by the ton. But like you I am looking to do something more worthwhile with my life."

"Bravo! Well, we shall look at this together and you can decide if you think I should take it on before I give Fiona my decision."

The inside of the Range Rover was sumptuous and the interior was cream leather, yet Liz was sure now this wasn't the car Ben had picked her up in as she certainly didn't remember having had to climb to get into it.

"I think this is a new car since we first met?"

"Well, yes, I had a BM before but I decided if I'm to live in the country then I need a four-wheel drive for the bad weather. Do you like it?"

"Who wouldn't? It's fabulous, and at least I haven't ruined the interior with my soaking wet clothes. I feel terrible about that. I was also very embarrassed about the smell of my soaking wet duffle coat."

"Don't be daft; you didn't do any harm to it. It's a car – that's what they are for, for goodness sake. I nearly suggested you bring Barnie but I don't quite know what the site is going to be like so I thought better of it."

"Barnie? In a brand new Range Rover with cream leather interior? Are you mad? I could never, ever bring myself to put his muddy body in such a gorgeous car. I even use a blanket in the back of my old van so that he doesn't lie on the clean dust sheets."

They chatted comfortably until the sat-nav began to direct them down a rough track then over a hill. Then they suddenly came upon the most impressive fortress of a building, and what looked like the remains of a garden. The garden, which had once obviously surrounded the castle, had long overgrown but it looked as though the ha-ha that had been used in the landscape gardening to keep the livestock out of the garden while providing an uninterrupted view still remained intact.

"Oh, how exquisite, I can't wait to mooch around. And you call this work?"

As Ben parked the Range Rover and opened the rear door he rummaged around in the back then suddenly handed Liz a coat hanger.

"This is for that lovely, but unsuitable coat, and this is what you need to wear for your own safety and my insurance."

Ben handed Liz a bright fluorescent-yellow safety jacket and a matching hard hat. When Liz fastened the zip on the coat, and put the matching hard hat on her head, she took one look in the wing mirror of the car. She closed her eyes, creased with embarrassment.

“I look like an oompaloompa.”

Her little legs in her tight black jeans and knee-length boots made her look like a giant lemon with legs. As Ben came around to her side of the car and unfortunately laughed out loud at her strange look, Liz pulled a funny pose and a face to match. And they both laughed – a lot.

“Well, there is one thing – if you get lost they would see you from space, but I bet you’re warm? So that’s all that matters.”

“So why does yours look smart and businesslike, and it makes you look all manly, whereas mine makes me look like something from a fruit stall?”

That set them off laughing again, before Ben asked, “Do I?”

"Do you what?"

"Look all manly in my jacket and helmet?"

"Oh, stop fishing, of course you do. You know fine you do, and I bet you have all the lassies after you?"

"Well, that's where you're wrong, but thank you, miss oompaloompa for those kind words."

They walked towards the imposing and statuesque building, and it was almost palpable, the feeling that the previous owners of such a place must have been very important clans people, the lairds of all they surveyed. As they began to walk around and in and out of what remained of the building, it was all too clear that it would take an awful lot of money to restore this castle to its former glory. Ultimately it would depend on how much money the current owner had to spend. Anything could be restored for a price.

On closer inspection Ben said that the walls and the roof were intact, some of the floors or ceilings had fallen in, but that it wasn't a major problem. The winter sun shone in brilliant shafts through the remaining windows, which still had the beautifully coloured stained glass in them. Liz stood in one of those shafts of sunlight and felt the slight warmth on her face. Closing her eyes, she could almost imagine what it must have been like, all those hundreds of years ago, to have stood in this very room, eyes closed and the sun on your face. With a good imagination you could almost hear the sounds of the past inhabitants, the chieftain's loud voice calling to his dogs, and the patter of their paws on the wooden floors, maidservants all clattering around the corridors.

"How lucky you are to make a decision as to whether the property is worth saving or not. It must be very hard."

"Oh, I'm afraid it doesn't work quite like that. This is the owner's property – they've bought it, whether I say anything or not.

They simply want to know if what they would like to do with it can be achieved, and at what price. I need to know if it's possible to save the building and incorporate everything they would like, with some suggestions from me as to how or if that can be achieved and at what price. It's a sort of meeting of minds, and if you can work with the owner and them with you then you are halfway there.

"What do you think of it? Would you save it?"

"Oh my goodness me, yes… I would lovingly restore every brick with the original stone if I could afford it. Oh just think what you could do with a place like this, and the panoramic views are spectacular. Do you think there is enough of it left to restore within a reasonable budget? I mean how much do you think something like this could cost to restore?"

"Well, now you're asking. Without a more in-depth search of the foundations and the roof timbers, you have to be talking two hundred and fifty to three hundred K, and that doesn't include however much the owner has already paid. I'll know more when I have some searches done on the land and the state of the stonework. However, in my opinion, the castle is definitely worth saving and I agree with you – it will be spectacular.

"I haven't actually met the owner yet, so I have no idea what type of person he or she is. I don't know yet if they want it to be a family home or a hotel, or a tourist attraction. They may want to renovate it in a modern style, or they may want to take it that step further and go completely contemporary."

To this Liz pulled a disapproving expression of disgust.

"However, I'm afraid I am only asked initially for my expert opinion on possibility and price. Then, if the client decides to take me on as the architect, only then do they tell you what they would like it to look like and you tell them if it's possible."

They had a final look round and the light was just beginning to fade as they slowly walked back towards the car. Liz was cold but very happy. She had really enjoyed the experience of imagining what could be done with such a building. She had enjoyed being with Ben and having a proper conversation about something important and meaningful for a change. This was what Liz meant when she told herself she needed a challenge, something that gave her a similar buzz.

"I've had a wonderful day, thank you so much for inviting me."

"You have?" Ben could see that Liz was completely serious, adding, "Well, you're very welcome to come again. If I accept the job, and the client likes what I report, then I will be up here regularly. Now give me your oompaloompa suit and hat and we'll go and find somewhere nice to eat. I'm starving, how about you?"

Ben brought the car to a stop in the car park of an out of the way little pub, which he quite obviously knew was here as it was off the beaten track. As they sat in front of a roaring open fire, they chatted easily and were amazed as the time simply flew by. It was Liz who eventually said she hoped Barnie had managed to cross his legs until she got home. The journey home went swiftly and, once outside Liz's cottage as they sat in the dark with the engine ticking gently over, Ben reached over and took one of Liz's hands.

"Thank you for coming with me today. I'm so glad I had the inspirational idea to ask you."

"Well, that was pure luck, you finding me on the common with Barnie."

"Uh-oh, no, I have a confession. I actually hoped you would be on the common with Barnie, and I intended to ask you to come with me today."

"Really? You should have just rung me, I would have come. I've really, really enjoyed every minute of it."

Ben pulled Liz's hand, bringing her close to his lips, which he placed slowly but firmly on to her slightly open mouth. He kissed firmly but gently, taking his time as if savouring every second before he drew away.

"Oh, Lizy," Ben said, as he looked directly into Liz's soft brown eyes.

He was about to say something else when Liz said, "Well, you have probably just made Mrs Mangle's year, never mind week. All that time sitting on a hard chair at the window watching me and Nigel and Zilch… Then you come along and wow! I'd better go now, and thanks again for taking me, I've had a terrific day. And don't hesitate to ask me again, with or without Barnie."

As Liz reached the front door of her cottage Ben gave a little toot of the horn and off he went into the night, leaving Liz's thoughts in total disarray. She knew the only thing for it was to take Barnie out to the common in order to think things out as usual. She knew one thing – it was likely to be a very long walk for Barnie. As her mind replayed that kiss over and over and over, Liz knew she had never been kissed like that since Bob, and she had thought she never would be again. The thing was… She had really enjoyed it, if she were honest. She was already looking forward to the next time.

Chapter 20

The first thing Liz found when coming down the stairs, under the letter box in the hallway, was a scrap of paper. Now scraps of paper were ominous in a village because they usually meant an up-and-coming event, or a meeting, or a jumble sale et cetera. Whatever it was, it usually meant you were expected to attend. These pieces of paper were usually treated like unexploded bombs by Liz, because she always knew they would involve her in some way and in this case she was right again.

A meeting in the village hall tomorrow evening, which was Wednesday. Pity, thought Liz. If it had been a Tuesday or a Thursday she could have got herself excused. However, unfortunately, for Wednesday she couldn't really find a valid reason not to go. The purpose of the meeting, the notice went on, was to fill in a questionnaire as to what the inhabitants of the village thought was an important requirement in the general layout of the new building. At the bottom of Liz's note there was a p.s. from Nigel, which meant he had been the one to post it. He requested that Liz jot down some suggestions and come earlier than the seven thirty stated so that they could discuss her suggestions.

In other words, thought Liz, he wants me to come up with a questionnaire and more or less deal with the village while he walks around again with his blinking clipboard.

"Ohhwa, I thought I'd escaped. I should have known. Although, Ben's bound to have got a note also, so I suppose I would be working with him rather than Nigel… Unless, of course, Fiona is there, but no, Ben is doing the plans. Well, we shall see tomorrow evening."

When Liz and Isabel arrived at the Duck as usual on a Tuesday, Liz was a little disappointed not to see Ben's Range Rover. He may come later, of course, Liz reasoned, and naturally she realised that he didn't have to come at all… Only she had kind of hoped he would.

The night flew past as it always did but Ben didn't turn up so Liz presumed he had been busy with other things. Angus and Isabel gravitated towards each other during the break; and even during the performance Liz saw Isabel watching Angus with a look in her eye she hadn't noticed before.

At the end of the night Angus helped to load Liz's instruments into her van. Then, feeling a little like a gooseberry but not minding in the least, Liz feigned a yawn, saying if she didn't get to bed soon she would sleep standing up.

"So I'll be off. No doubt I'll see you both at the meeting tomorrow night?"

Liz could see Angus and Isabel look at each other in a conspiratorial way until eventually they both blurted out together, "Well, actually, we won't be able to make it, we're, er…" stammered Isabel.

"We're going out for a meal. I've already booked it and I'm not going to cancel it for one of—"

"Niiigel's boring meetings" they both said in unison.

Liz's grin started at one side of her face then broke into a huge smile, saying she hoped they had a wonderful time and to hell with Nigel's meeting.

"Oh, you're a little good'un," said Angus. "We knew you'd understand; we just don't want all and sundry to know, that's all."

"Hey, your secret is safe with me."

On Wednesday morning Liz knew she had her last job before the Christmas holidays, which was a tiny little kitchen at the Mill. Mrs Johnson was all ready for her when she arrived at her flat. She even had her own dust sheets covering the worktops.

"I thought I'd save a little bit time for you when you came, Liz. I'm afraid I'll have to nip out, if that's all right? I seem to have run out of my painkillers… Oh, it's such a nuisance because I am positive I put them in the cupboard and I even ticked them off my list on the calendar to say I had them… Twenty-eight tablets and they should have lasted me up until I order my last box to cover me over Christmas… I don't suppose you could have a look for me, Liz? You know sometimes you can be looking at something and not see it, if you know what I mean."

Liz stood on a stool to look into the wall cupboard where Kate kept the old ice cream carton in which she kept her tablets. Liz could see it was very unlikely that she would have made such a mistake as the remaining tablets in the box were almost alphabetically placed. Kate was certainly not old or infirm; she simply had chronic arthritis, which meant that she was crippled with pain most of the time. She knew all too well how bad the pain would get if she did forget her medication; therefore both Liz and Kate felt there had to be an explanation for the missing tablets.

"Well, I'm sorry, Kate, there are no tablets up there other than the ones you know about. Listen, let me get this little bit of emulsioning done for you then I'll go and see McLeish and bring your tablets back for you."

"Oh no, no, Liz, I couldn't ask that of you, no, really."

"Listen, I was going to call at McLeish's anyway – I need something myself so it's not a problem. You go and have a sit down and I'll only be a couple of hours, so don't worry – we'll get them long before he closes."

As Liz was finishing off in the kitchen she couldn't help but think that, although the Mill was for the elderly, the people she knew were all perfectly compos mentis. It might have been true that as you got older you tended to forget things occasionally, but not to the extent that she had come across just in the last two weeks of working at the Mill. No, she thought, there has to be a reason, and I am getting a bad feeling about this, but I won't say anything until I have had a word with McLeish himself.

Liz packed her ladders into the van, then washed her paintbrushes and placed them in her bucket, saying she would be back in two shakes to Kate and she was not to worry as Liz would get to the bottom of it for her. Kate relaxed a little but was agitated at the fact that she was convinced she hadn't made a mistake and was furious with herself for misplacing her tablets, which was the only explanation she could think of.

Liz caught McLeish himself and she popped her head around the counter so that she could ask him quietly if he had noticed a strange amount of extra tablets being ordered or requested for the Mill lately.

"Well, do you know, Liz, it's funny you should say that. I was just saying to Judy what a lot of extra medications I have given out to the Mill lately. Especially the painkillers and sleeping tablets, such as tramadol, diclofenac, erm, hang on, I'll get my book. I have begun to take note because I actually thought to myself what a lot of 'lost tablets' there have been lately.

"Yes, here it is – Iona McLaughlin lost her tramadol and naproxen. Minnie McDonald needed more mogadon, yet she had just been issued with twenty-eight and she claims she only takes them when she can't sleep. Hannah Burns needed more diclofenac and she also needed more mogadon, yet I've never known her need more than one or two boxes in a year before. The ones I was really concerned about were Mrs Martin's – she has been prescribed benzodiazepine for when she really has a bad time and can't get any sleep but not to be taken on a regular basis at all as it is addictive and she knows this very well."

"Well," Liz told him, "actually I've come about another missing prescription, that of Mrs Johnson, Kate. She appears to be very methodical in keeping her tablets. I checked the box myself and she had actually ticked them off on her calendar, a prescription for twenty-eight days. Then she has the days counted from now until Christmas when she needs to order her new supply. I have checked and double-checked and they are definitely not there. The thing is, Mr McLeish, I know these old ladies as well as you do and they are not senile – forgetful sometimes, maybe, but all of them? Not all at the same time. There is something very funny going on here and I'm beginning to have my suspicions but I dare not say anything until I have more proof.

"I would be grateful if you would give me another prescription in the meantime. Then I will mention it to a friend of mine and see what they say. I feel a lot better now that I know it's not just the oldies and me that thinks they are going daft."

When Liz got back to Kate's and gave her the medication, she was so relieved. It angered Liz to think that these poor old dears were so worried about asking for more painkillers or sleeping tablets. If they needed them, why shouldn't they simply be able to have them? In fact, she was a little annoyed about the whole thing, and she was beginning to add two and two together.

"Kate, do you see much of Mrs Monroe? Does she call in very often to see you?" Liz attempted to sound nonchalant in her enquiry.

"Well, to be honest, I don't see her much during the day. She always seems to come when I'm either in bed or having a shower. She seems to come at the most inconvenient times, if you know what I mean. And she lets herself in with her pass key. Now that's not right, you know, Liz, she shouldn't do it. I don't mean to be unfriendly or unkind, but, to be honest, Liz, I'm not very fond of Mrs Monroe.

"There's something about her… Oh, I shouldn't be saying this, but that son of hers is a bad lot and he's always hanging about at the back door. I can see him out of my window. I'm a little afraid he might see me one of these days. He comes and bangs on the door until she opens it and then they argue, argue something terrible they do… In fact, I've seen him threatening her. I'm not sure what he's saying, but he has a nasty face when he's shouting right close to her, real close, you know… Oh, he gives me the creeps."

"Well, I wouldn't worry about it, Kate. Just you stay out of his way; I'm sure he isn't interested in the likes of you. I'm glad we got your kitchen done and your tablets sorted, and I hope you have a lovely Christmas."

"Thank you, Liz, I don't know what we would do without the likes of you, and your kindness. It's a weight off my shoulders now, and I'll put these tablets somewhere safe. All the very best of the season to you and your boy – Tom, isn't it?"

Liz was absolutely positive now, positive that Mrs Monroe had something to do with all the missing tablets – her and her pass key. How dare she? But… Liz knew she couldn't simply accuse her – she needed proof and she had to tell someone, she couldn't keep this to herself. She would see Angus on Thursday night – he would know what to do.

Chapter 21

Liz arrived early for the village meeting as requested by Nigel. And she had been right, of course – as soon as she arrived she was more or less jumped on by Nigel, who had brought a laptop and printer that he had borrowed from the school. Liz was expected to prepare a questionnaire in less than forty-five minutes, which she would then have to print off as many times as people walked through the door. Nigel, meanwhile, would walk around straightening chairs and chatting with all and sundry as they arrived. Namely Fiona and Ben, one would suppose, if they came.

Liz was rushed to the table with the laptop, and more or less put to work. Well, I suppose it's no hardship, thought Liz. For goodness sake, it's simple enough, and it is for the village. Then I suppose I give one out to each person who will fill it in then put it in the basket on the table. What's wrong with that? Nothing, she thought, it was just the fact that she was being roped in again by Niiigel… Oh God, she was doing it herself now, saying Niiigel like Isabel and everyone else.

It was a simple enough task – a single foolscap sheet of paper, not too long or too boring, just enough so that people were allowed to have their say about their village hall.

1. How large or small should the building be?

2. What kind of heating? Suggestions…

3. As different functions require different rooms, how many rooms do you think the hall would need?

4. Who do you think should represent the users of the village hall – the parish council or a separate committee? Would you want elections to choose village hall representatives if the parish council is not chosen?

5. If we have a kitchen, should it only be large enough to serve drinks, or should it be a fully functioning kitchen equipped for catering?

6. What kind of utilities should the village go for – electricity, gas, or solar power?

Once she had completed the questionnaire she printed a pile, then she simply sat at the table by the entrance and handed them out as people entered. She had given quite a few out and said hello to almost everyone as they had come in without even looking up, most of the time, when a familiar voice said hello and she actually looked up into his smiling face and floppy hair.

Ben leant down to whisper conspiratorially, "I see you've been roped in again. Where's Nigel? Oh, I see him. He's inside with his clipboard. Oops, too late, he's seen me."

"Ha ha, I've done my bit. It's you and Fiona he wants now."

Just as Liz said it she realised that Fiona was at her elbow, giving her a very predatory look. It was quite obvious that she didn't like the fact that Ben had leaned in to talk to Liz in such a friendly way.

"Oh, hello, Fiona, I didn't see you there. I was just saying I think Nigel is looking for you both," Liz said, hoping that she sounded as though she hadn't understood the look. You never know, she thought, Fiona may just assume she was a country bumpkin of a decorator and no threat after all. Mmm, so that's definitely the way the wind blows, thought Liz. I wonder if it blows both ways.

The meeting went on and on as usual and by the time everyone had filled in the questionnaire and Nigel had given yet another speech it was much later than she had hoped before she could slip away unnoticed, which she did as soon as she had collected the last of the forms. She placed them in a neat little pile on Nigel's table when he was still on the platform speaking. And, without a glance at Ben and Fiona, Liz slipped out.

The following morning Liz decided she had better go to the supermarket and stock up for Tom coming home at the weekend. Then, as she thought about Mrs Monroe, she knew she would have to speak to someone and Angus would be at work until later so she may as well tell him at the Duck, but Isabel would be at home and she needed to talk to someone about it.

As she drove towards the supermarket she passed Ben's entryway and her eyes automatically slid upwards past the main stone pillars and the open gate towards the house. Her heart missed a beat as she saw both Ben's Range Rover and Fiona's Honda sporty coupé. And it was obvious as the windows were still frosted that they had both stood outside all night.

Liz parked the van in the supermarket car park and wandered round mindlessly pushing a trolley. She hadn't any idea what on earth she was dropping in as she walked up and down several aisles. She told herself she had no right to care who Ben had staying overnight in his home. But she couldn't help being a little…jealous? Oh God, surely not.

"What a stupid woman I am!" Liz said to herself. "I never wanted to love anyone, ever, after Bob, and then… I seem to… Well, that's ridiculous; it's a crush, that's all it can be, for goodness sake. I hardly know the man."

"Excuse me?" said a total stranger who had thought Liz was speaking to them. Liz apologised immediately and pushed her trolley purposefully in the opposite direction.

Oh pull yourself together woman, she told herself. So, a good-looking man showed you a little interest, and he took you to a castle and gave you a meal and a kiss. A kiss, a wonderful meaningful kiss… Struth, woman.

Just as she was remonstrating with herself for being so daft, she pushed her trolley into the back of a tall young man, who luckily thought she was a bit simple, talking to herself and bumping into people, so he gave her a dirty look and stormed off, limping where she had rammed her trolley into his ankles.

By the time Liz had filled the back of her van with enough food to feed an army if Tom was to bring one home with him for the Christmas holidays, Liz had decided tha tshe would nip to Isabel's. She would have at least an hour and a half before any frozen food began to drip all over the van.

She was unprepared for the surprise awaiting her when she arrived. She knocked on the door in her usual waking the dead sort of way and let herself into the entrance porch where normally the passage door would be unlocked at this time of the morning. However, it was still locked. Liz assumed then that Isabel had gone out shopping so was on the point of leaving when a rather sheepish Isabel came down the stairs and Liz could quite clearly see through the glass door that she still had her dressing gown on.

"Wow, you're late this morning, girl, it must have been a good night last night. I might add, while I was slaving away at the village hall and covering for your absence."

Liz was in full throttle when she realised that there was a pair of men's shoes at the bottom of the stairs. And just as the thought process began to kick in, it suddenly dawned on her that she was intruding and that Isabel wasn't alone. She began to rapidly backtrack, saying she had better go and she would see her later at the Duck.

"Erm, sorry…"

"S'okay," said Isabel with a sly grin on her face. She certainly wasn't going to ask Liz to stay, even out of good manners – to hell with that. They both smothered a laugh as Liz backed away and into her van and off in a fit of the giggles.

Chapter 22

After she had put all her shopping away and boiled the kettle for a coffee, Liz knew it would be no good. She wouldn't be able to think about anything else until she had spoken to someone about the Mill. She decided to ring her mother. Her down-to-earth approach may be a bit earthy, to say the least, but she said it like it was, so to speak.

"Hello, darling, what's wrong? You never phone in the middle of the day unless there is something wrong, now what is it?"

"Hello, Mum, how are you? Oh, I'm fine, and you?"

"Sorry, darling, how are you? And I'm fine. Now tell me what's wrong."

"Okay, listen and I'll tell you. Oh, it may be nothing, but I can't help thinking about it and I need someone else's opinion. Now,

Mum, try to be objective and don't jump to conclusions, okay? Right, well, the top and bottom of it is I've been doing a lot of decorating work at the Mill, you know, the sheltered place? Well," Liz went on, a little uncertainly, "each of the old dears I've been working for appears to have 'misplaced' some of their tablets. Even though they were positive they had got them, it was obvious they weren't there even when I searched. It seems to have been happening far more often than normal, even allowing for forgetfulness, so I had a word with Mr McLeish. It turns out he is also beginning to see that he has been prescribing a lot of what he describes as 'lost tablets'. So he has decided to keep a record of the types of medicine that are going missing."

"And let me guess – they are all heavy painkillers, and sleepers, moggies and diazepam and probably bennies."

"Mum, you sound like the Artful Dodger, where do you get your street language from?"

"Years of living abroad, dear, and hearing what goes on among an ageing pill-popping community. You've got a thief. Not only a thief, but they know who has what meds and they have access to the building. So who does that tell you it is? I'll tell you who – it has to be the warden. They are the only person who can gain access to each of the flats. Who is the warden?"

"Well, you know her, Mum, it's Mrs Monroe, but I heard…"

"Oh yes, I know who you mean, and she has a son. He'll be in his late twenties, early thirties maybe – a bad lot, a thoroughly bad lot, always was. There's your answer, girl, that's who's filching your pills. Well, at least she is, and he will be selling them. What do the residents think of her? Is she well liked?"

"Well, actually, no, not really. They say she never organises anything, you know day trips or whatever, and they only ever see her either early in the morning when they are still in bed or late at night, also when they are in bed. And… They don't like the fact that she uses her pass key and just walks in."

"There is your answer in a nut shell, I'm afraid. What a shame it's happening in a wonderful place like the Mill, with lovely village people in, and a good wage to boot. I bet there isn't a lot of work involved."

"No, they can do as much or as little as they want. However, in Mrs Monroe's case it means none by the sounds of it. And she gets a wonderful flat free of charge. Mum, we are digressing. What shall I do about it? Knowing or suspecting someone isn't the same as having concrete proof so I can't go to the police, now, can I?"

"No, darling, you need to set a trap of some sort. You need to catch her in the act. If you catch her she'll spill about her son; she'll not take the fall on her own."

"Oh, Mum, where do you get your language from? You sound like a drug lord one minute with bennies and moggies and then a street cop the next with your 'taking the fall'. But you're right, of course."

"You're darn toot'n I'm right. Over here when they suspect anyone they place hidden cameras and catch them in the act. You could do that, couldn't you? You could let it be known that, say, er, one of your oldies was having, for example, a month's supply of drugs delivered. You could sort of let it slip as you're talking to her that you have been asked to collect them for the old dear and er, well, you must know someone who could help you?"

"Well, actually, Angus's mother is in the Mill now, did you know?"

"Oh no, poor old dear, I didn't know."

"Mum, there's only about ten years' difference between you and Iona. Anyway, Angus will be at the Duck tonight and I was going to ask him anyway what he thought about my suspicions. But you're right, you have been very helpful, if a little colourful as usual. Yes, I think I'll ask Angus if we could do some sort of surveillance. What do you think?"

"Yes, definitely, I wish I was there. If I lived in one of those flats I would give you permission, I would love it. I would pretend I was asleep and catch them in the act."

"Oh God, Mum, you are getting worse. You are becoming even battier the older you get, but I can imagine you organising a gang of oldies to catch her."

"You know, Liz, you've hit the nail on the head. I need something to occupy me, I need a purpose, and I love to organise. If I were a warden I would organise dances. Tea dances in the afternoon to bring in outsiders, Bingo, whist tournaments. Oh, I would bring that place to life."

"Do you mean that, Mum? Would you come back if there was a vacancy?"

"Well, I wouldn't like anyone to think we were framing the old broad so that I could take her place, but yes, yes, I certainly would come back. You get a nice little flat and I would be close to you."

"But not too close, thank goodness! No, I didn't mean that, Mum, it would be lovely to have you back. But in the meantime I'll talk to Angus and tell you what he suggests. So just don't start packing yet, okay? And, Mum, thanks. Bye."

"Bye, sista, I'll be waiting by the phone," Florence said with a flourish before putting her phone down.

Liz couldn't stop laughing – her mother always managed to make her laugh, she was such a character. To tell the truth, she missed her a great deal. The phone was a wonderful invention but it would be lovely to have her closer.

Chapter 23

When Liz arrived at the Duck and was busy unpacking her instruments from the car she could see Isabel locking her door and hurrying over towards her. Giving each other nudges and winks, Isabel tried to look sheepish but unfortunately she didn't succeed. In fact she looked positively glowing.

"Sorry about this morning, Isabel, I didn't give it a thought. Anyway, in a roundabout way, it was Angus I wanted to speak to but I think he was otherwise occupied… So I gather you had a good night? Oops, sorry, that's not what I meant. I gather you had an enjoyable meal out, then you had a good night?"

"Ha ha, you horror, yes we had a lovely meal, then a greaaat night… Oh, Liz, he is so kind and gentle and completely different to the rotters I'm used to. In fact, some of the things he says, I have to look twice to see if he is being sarcastic. Then I realise he's not, he is actually just a nice man."

"I could have told you that a long time ago, I just didn't think he was your type. I'm so glad you two have hit it off, but why after all this time?"

"Do you know, Liz, I think I've eventually grown up. I think each time I got married it was for the wrong reasons, and in each of my fly-by-night husbands I saw one characteristic I liked. If I could have rolled them all into one person he would have been the perfect man. And do you know I'm almost terrified to think it, but I feel that Angus was what I was looking for all along, and I haven't felt this happy for a very, very long time or so optimistic about my future. You know, Liz, I was beginning to imagine that I'd had my chance and I was destined to go into old age alone, and that is a frightening thought."

"I am so pleased for you, Isabel, and I'm sure that this is the one. Angus is a gentle giant of a man and he is everything you could want. Speaking of Angus, though, I need to talk to him urgently."

"Oh, don't go telling him anything I've been saying, Liz, for God's sake."

"Don't be silly; it's not about you, surprisingly enough." Liz laughed at Isabel's face, which looked incredulous that other things were going on in the world at this precise moment that didn't involve her. "Come inside – we've got half an hour before starting time, which should be just enough to tell you what I've found out."

All three of them sat in the corner of the Duck furtively whispering, like in a scene from a film, but certainly like nothing they were ever likely to have been involved in before. It seemed incredible in the sleepy little village of Juniper that such things could go on in the outside world that not Angus, Isabel or Liz had ever come across in their sheltered lives before.

"So what do you think, Angus? Is it possible to place some sort of camera in your mum's flat, or do you think it's too dangerous? If you do, just say so and I'll think of something else. I wouldn't want to involve either you or your mum, or anyone else for that matter, in something that could be dangerous. Oh, I wish my mother were here – she would do it like a flash. She was quite miffed that she couldn't get involved as she is too far away."

"Actually," said Angus, "you'd be surprised what my mum will do; she's a feisty old bird. I knew there was something funny going on with the tablets – it just didn't occur to me what it was. God, when I think of that woman just going into mother's flat and stealing while she was asleep, or whenever, it makes my blood fair boil. No, don't you think twice about it, we're in. We'll go and have a word with Mother and let her know all about it, but don't worry – she'll be game for it, I'm sure."

Isabel chimed in then. "Listen, I've got a video camera that I bought for my holiday in America and I've hardly ever used it but it's in perfect working order if that's any good?

Shall I take it with us when we go to your mother's and we could try to find a place to hide it?"

"Oh, good idea, Isabel," Liz said. "Oh, Mum will be so envious when I tell her. It was her idea, you know, to use a hidden camera. Honestly, I think her previous life must have been in the underworld."

"Right, so we'll go tomorrow morning and see Mother and think more on the details then. Now I think we should be starting. In case you haven't noticed, the room is filling up and we are creating a bit of a stir just sitting here. We look as though we are plotting a strike," said Angus in his broad Scottish accent, which always made him sound like a skirted clansman of days gone by.

It was agreed that Liz wouldn't go with them to the Mill in case Mrs Monroe should see them all together. It would give the game away. However, a normal visit from Angus and his lady friend wouldn't, so that's what they planned to do.

Chapter 24

Liz was beside herself to know what had happened at the Mill. After having taken Barnie for his morning run on the common, she made her way home. All the time she had been out, part of her had hoped that she would bump into Ben as she had before. However, he had been conspicuous by his absence since the morning she had seen both his and Fiona's cars on his drive.

She had just had time to boil the kettle when Angus and Isabel arrived together looking all excited. Angus had decided to take the day off as this was more important, he said.

"Well, my mother is so excited, and certainly wants in on the plan. She was furious at the fact that Mrs Monroe has had her thinking she was beginning to go senile, and to think she had been stealing from her flat by using her key made her very angry indeed."

Isabel had told Iona about the camera and they had taken a good look around the flat to decide where it should be concealed.

“The problem is that Mother keeps her tablets in the bathroom cabinet and really there’s no place to hide the camera in there. Also, we somehow have to let Mrs Monroe know about the extra tablets.”

“Well, how about I say that I need to go back to Iona’s to do a little job and while I’m there I’ll do what I often do, which is to collect more tablets from McLeish’s, but this time I’ll let it slip in front of Mrs Monroe and, erm, I’ll make up something elaborate, such as that her month’s supply is too big for the cabinet so I’ve put it in the kitchen cupboard or something like that, what do you think?”

“Yesss, sort of. We don’t want her to guess or be too obvious, but yes, everyone knows you do collect prescriptions so that’s believable. But you’re not usually so careless about telling anyone where they’re kept. Although you could actually say to

Mrs Monroe that you think my mother is definitely beginning to lose her marbles and thought you had better tell her where her extra supply of tablets is in case the need arises. What do you think?"

"That's excellent. You had better clear that with your mother, though, or she'll go mad, ha ha."

"Och, she's fine. Her bark's worse than her bite."

"Well, I'll take your word for it. Right, I think that's an excellent plan. Tell her to let it be known that I'm coming to give her little kitchen a quick spruce up before Christmas and I'll have a good scout round in the kitchen to see where I can hide the camcorder. The thing is it will have to be switched on each night or it will run out of tape, won't it?"

"Well, actually, I think it has some sort of sensor on, which only activates when it senses movement. If I remember rightly, basically that's the reason I never used it – I didn't really understand it," said Isabel.

"Oh, that's excellent, then; it saves having to worry about resetting it as we have no idea how long it will take for Mrs Monroe to take the bait. So if your mum just switches it on at the wall socket when she goes to bed, that will surely be enough tape. I rather hope she'll take the bait earlier rather than later, though, although I'm sure she'll want to get her son off her back as soon as possible. He seems quite an angry man, judging by the look of him last time I saw him with his mum outside the Mill. Right, so, Angus, how about you tell your mum to let it be known that I am going to do her decorating on Monday, just to do a half-day spruce up in the kitchen. Then I'll do the rest. I'll have to make it my business to bump into Mrs Monroe, and plant the seed that your mum is going a bit dotty, hide the camera and the tablets and Bob's your uncle."

"It all sounds very easy but we have to keep our fingers crossed that she takes the bait more or less straight away or we will all be nervous wrecks, including your mother, Angus."

"Oh, don't you worry about her, she's a tough old bird. Just let us know when you've planted the stuff."

"Ha ha, my mother would absolutely love all this. You should hear her, she sounds like something from *The Bill*. She's even up on all the jargon – moggies, bennies – you should hear her. She even wants to come back and run the place when this is all over. In fact, if she had been here she would have organised the whole thing in order to ensure she got the job, ha ha."

Chapter 25

Liz decided that after she had taken Barnie for his early morning walk she would call and collect her fresh Christmas tree from the village shop and spend this Saturday morning organising her and Tom's Christmas. He had called to say he was having a couple of days with friends in Edinburgh now that he had started his break but that he would be home by Friday, which Liz reminded herself would be the twenty-first. She couldn't believe it – where had the time gone? The months were simply flying by.

She parked her little van on the edge of the common and let Barnie out of the back doors. Anyone watching would have thought him an old man, the way he sauntered out of the back, but, once he was on level ground, if he saw a rabbit in the distance he was off like a greyhound at the track. When she returned home, it appeared that Isabel had called and left her camcorder in the porch with a note saying she hoped she had better luck than her, understanding the instructions that had quite clearly never been out of the box. This spoke volumes about Isabel.

Liz decided she would attempt that later. First of all she was going to tackle the Christmas tree. By the time she had dragged the tree inside the porch, sorted the stand out from the shed and reached into the loft hatch for the decorations, she was shattered. But, not one to be deterred, she was sat on the floor inside the porch, wrestling with a very sharp, spiky tree in an attempt to fit the stand when there was a tap on the porch door. As Liz looked up she couldn't have been more surprised to see anyone at her door.

"Hi, are you busy, or is that a silly question?" asked Ben.

Liz separated herself from her spiky tree and leaned over to open the door.

"Hi, er, hello, what are you doing here? Sorry, come in if you can get in, I'm just in the middle of…"

"I can see. Can I give you a hand? You look as though you need a spare one."

"Well, if you don't mind, you could actually just hold it upright while I try to fit the stand. It has a sort of screw thing at the bottom. The old chap in the shop said they are much easier than filling a tub with soil but I can't see how."

"Listen, why don't you hold the top and I'll put the stand on? I've seen these before – actually they are very good and much less messy and more secure. There, done. Now where do you want it?"

"You mean that's it? I've been on the floor for ages and my hands are all scratched from the pines. I'm normally quite practical. Actually, er, if you could just bring it through by the fireside… Yes, that's lovely, just there."

"Can I help any more? Are you going to decorate it? I'd love to help – I haven't done that in years."

"Wow, you must be bored if that's what turns you on, as Tom would say. Yes, you certainly can help. In fact, you can start by checking the lights. Have you noticed that when you put the lights away they are fine, but when you take them out the following year they don't work? Now what's that all about? I mean who tampered with them during the year?"

"Ha ha, leave the lights to me. You go and make us a coffee, if that's not being too forward."

Liz went and made them both a well-earned coffee and as she came through to the living room the lights were already twinkling on the tree. Although nude of decorations, already it looked festive.

"Hey, you cheated, or you were lucky, because if I had done the lights I would have sat with a bag of spare bulbs checking every one, and it would have taken me hours."

As they began to decorate the tree Ben began by telling Liz he had been to Edinburgh for a few days on business.

"Oh, and by the way I've taken the contract for the Muir of Orchil castle. The client is a software coder so apparently money is no object. They are the golden words Fiona likes to hear, but 'create away' are the words I like and the client is very happy for me to put my stamp on it as long as his certain requirements are met. Fiona is quite happy that I do the large time-taking work as she much prefers the bread and butter fast-earning contracts. I like to look upon the contracts I take as challenging, creative, and most of all pleasurable."

"Well, if you're lucky enough to pick and choose, I couldn't agree more… Oh, hang on."

The phone had begun ringing, and as Liz picked it up, before she could tell Isabel she wasn't alone, Isabel was asking if the camcorder was what she needed. Would it do the job?

"I don't know, Isabel, I haven't even had it out of the box, but if it's as large as the box it's not going to be very easy to conceal inconspicuously, but I'll let you know. No, of course I haven't read the instructions yet. How could I? I haven't had a chance. Listen, erm, I have Ben here and we are at present putting up my Christmas tree. Can I get back to you later? Yes, I did say Ben, and no, you're not interrupting anything, but I will ring you later after I've had a chance to look at the camcorder, okay?"

Liz put down the phone then she looked at Ben, wondering if she should bother attempting to explain her very odd conversation with Isabel, when he said, "Erm, camcorder? Conceal? What on earth? Are you a super spy or something? Don't tell me you're Wonder Woman! No, excuse me for saying this, but you are a little on the small side to be Wonder Woman. Although don't get me wrong, I don't mean that in a figure sense. I mean it in the height sense, erm…"

"Stop. Before you dig yourself any deeper, I know what you mean, and no, I'm not Wonder Woman. Listen, er, I don't really know if I should tell you this, and if I do you have to keep it a complete secret, I've already told two other people.

"We – and that is not the royal we, it's the Angus, Isabel, my mother and me we – believe that Mrs Monroe at the Mill sheltered housing is stealing drugs from the elderly people and giving them to her son, who in turn we presume is selling them on the open market. We can't simply report her to the police – we need proof – so we've hatched a plan to catch her in the act, so to speak. Hence the camcorder, which belongs to Isabel, and I have to first of all figure out how to use it. Then hide it in Iona's – that's Angus's mother's – kitchen and hope to catch Mrs Monroe in the act of pinching the drugs."

Ben was sat on the floor with a look of disbelief on his face, still holding a Christmas bauble, which he had been about to place on the tree.

"You are kidding me? This isn't for real? You are not really going to attempt this without telling the police, are you?"

"Yes, don't you see? We can't go to the police yet; we have no proof and she would just get away with it."

"But this is dangerous stuff; this is drugs. I can't believe it – drugs in this wonderful, idyllic little village."

"Firstly, drugs are everywhere. Just because we live in a village doesn't mean we don't have the same things as they have in the city. We do but on a smaller scale. You'd be surprised at what happens in a village. The only difference is that in a village we try to stamp it out as quickly as we can before it takes hold. But in the city things grow like a mushroom and it's difficult to find the root.

"And secondly, there's no danger involved. Honestly, all I'm going to do is pretend to do a little bit of decorating in Iona's kitchen and put what I will let Mrs Monroe know is a month's supply of her medication into the wall cupboard, which will explain why they are not in her bathroom cabinet as normal, because there wouldn't be room. Also there wasn't anywhere to hide a camera in there so we devised a new plan to explain why the kitchen cupboard! Then I will hide the camcorder."

"Do you normally tell her where people's medicines are kept? Won't she think that's a bit of a giveaway?" Ben asked.

"No, we thought of that – she has already implied that some of the oldies are becoming a bit forgetful, in order to explain where their tablets were disappearing to. So I am going to tell her that Angus is a bit concerned about his mum becoming a little senile, losing her tablets and one thing and another. So we will say that we have got spare tablets for her in case she needs them over the Christmas period, but that we've had to put them in the kitchen cupboard as there are too many to fit into the bathroom cabinet.

"But I've got to first of all have a look at Isabel's camcorder then find a place to hide it in Iona's kitchen."

"But how on earth are you going to, well, work the camcorder, if you know what I mean? Won't the tape run out or something?"

"Well, Isabel says it has a movement sensor on it so it should only activate when someone is actually in the kitchen, but I have to read about it yet. I haven't actually had a look at it yet. I wanted to put my tree up first."

"Well, let's get the tree finished then and I'll help you sort out the camcorder."

"Are you sure? You sure you haven't got better things to do with your time, other than help me bait the trap, as my mother would say?"

“As long as you will do one thing for me, I’d absolutely love to help you out.”

“And what’s that?”

“Will you come with me again tomorrow and have another look at Muir Castle? I need to take some photographs and measurements in more detail.”

“I would absolutely love to come with you again, and you don’t have to bribe me, and you don’t have to get involved in our village ‘drugs bust’, ha ha. My mum will be kicking herself that she can’t be in at the ‘kill’, so to speak. She loves a good drama.”

“Your mother sounds like a very, very unusual woman, just like her daughter,” Ben said appreciatively. “Where is she then? I’m sure I would enjoy meeting her.”

“My mother? Oh, she lives in Benidorm. She retired there some years ago. She is a sun worshipper; although lately I’ve had the feeling that she misses all the scandal of village life, though not the English winters.

She would absolutely love to be here for this little Miss Marple encounter – there would be no holding her. She would want to be up to her neck in it."

"She sounds fascinating. Do you miss her?"

"Yes, actually I do. She can be a pain sometimes, and she is always trying to marry me off to someone – since Bob passed away, to anyone, actually. Any single male within a hundred miles would qualify. She hates loose ends and I'm now a loose end that needs to be dealt with before she pops her clogs, as she so crudely puts it."

By this time they had finished placing all the baubles on the tree and were clearing the empty storage boxes into the passage cupboard. The tree looked lovely – very festive in time for Tom's return.

"Come on then, get this camcorder out of the box. We had better try to figure out how it works before you do your clandestine bit. When are you going to do that then?"

"Monday. Angus has told Iona to let it be known, and I must say that when anyone has any work done in their flat the news travels like a plague of locusts, so by Monday it will be all round the building that I'm coming."

"I think I should come with you, to make sure…"

"No, no, you can't do that. Then it would be all around the building that a strange man had been in Iona's flat. No, that would never do, it would tip Mrs Monroe off."

"Oh, all right, as long as you promise that's all you're going to do. Nothing dangerous?"

Liz felt a pang of warmth that someone was watching over her, well, apart from her mum, Angus, Isabel, Tom, et cetera. No, someone male, masculine, and erm, nice-looking. In fact, thought Liz, someone she could really fancy. Who was she kidding? She fancied him like hell and she had from the very beginning.

They spent the next hour working out how the camcorder worked, and actually it wasn't that difficult. It did have a sensor on it and it was a wonderful idea – it meant that no one would have to keep turning the camera on or off but during the day Iona herself could turn it off while she was the only one in the kitchen. All Liz had to do was find a suitable place to hide it. After that it was all in the lap of the gods.

"Well now, that's done. I think I should take Barnie out for a walk if you fancy stretching your legs a little? I think we've earned a break."

"Agreed. I will come with you if you will have supper with me… Er, a takeaway in front of the fire by the tree, how about that?"

To Liz's ears it sounded perfect.

Chapter 26

They walked slowly round the common as Barnie tore around regardless of the fact that it was almost dark. There was something very relaxing about strolling along in the dusk – conversations became more explicit than would ever happen in broad daylight.

"So you say your mother would love to see you marry again. How do you feel about marrying again?"

"Oh, well, as I say, my mother wants me to be neatly and perfectly happy so she can stop worrying about me. She loved Bob, don't get me wrong. They got on like a house on fire. That's the problem. She knows what he would have wanted and she uses that against me. Bob wouldn't have wanted me to end up alone, she'll say, and she's right, he wouldn't."

"You must have had a wonderful relationship to know each other so well."

“We did. I’d known Bob since our school days and we were just somehow right for each other. We both loved music and, well, we had the same hobbies.”

“What did Bob die of, if that’s not too personal a question?”

“He died of liver cancer… God knows where he got that from, he was just unlucky. There didn’t seem to be any history of it in his family. We checked in case Tom had the gene, but we couldn’t find any. Just unlucky, I suppose. It was over very quickly, and yes, he and my mother kept telling me that I wasn’t to be on my own.”

“How would Tom feel about you remarrying, if ever?”

“Well, I don’t mean this in a cruel way, but I don’t think Tom would mind as long as it wasn’t…”

“Nigel” they both said in unison.

"I'm sorry about that," Liz continued, "but you see Nigel is a person who evokes a certain annoyance among those he meets. Well, you met him, you must have felt it. Yet when Bob died he filled my life with a sort of itinerary of what appeared to be important tasks, and although, basically, yes, I was doing his running around for him, it served its purpose. It helped me get through that numb time, the bit after Bob had gone. You see, when someone is ill you are running to and fro and you are needed. Then when they're gone, suddenly you're not needed any more. There's nowhere you need to be, no place you need to go. So I will always thank Nigel for filling in the gaps in my life after Bob. But marriage to Nigel – never. And you – why aren't you married, or is that too personal?"

"Never had time; never made time; it was never on my list of priorities. And, to be honest, I had begun to think that I had totally missed the proverbial boat. But you never know, stranger things have happened. I hope I have changed my lifestyle and seen the error of my ways before it was too late. I do sound a little like Ebenezer Scrooge, don't I? But I can assure you, I do 'keep Christmas in my heart' and I'm not mean. However, the overwork bit I must really work on if I'm to be saved."

"Well, I, for one, don't think you will spend your life alone, and I also believe you have seen the error of your ways."

"Oh, that's nice. Have you someone in mind?" Ben said this with a definite twinkle in his eye, which Liz saw as they were walking towards the street light on the edge of the common.

When they arrived back at the cottage Ben piled some logs on to the fire and pulled a small table over towards the sofa while Liz opened the wine in the kitchen. When she came back into the warm and cosy lounge she couldn't have been more pleasantly surprised.

"Mmm, it looks so cosy in here. I thought you might want to eat in the kitchen – I came through to ask before bringing in the wine."

"Well, if you don't mind, I thought it looked wonderful in here – the fire, the tree, and we can share and talk if that's okay with you?"

"Oh yes, that's definitely okay with me."

Score one to Ben, thought Liz, though she realised that if she were counting properly he would be almost up to ten – he loves dogs, he eats takeaways in front of the fire, he doesn't mind sharing, he loves the group. So far he ticks all my boxes, thought Liz.

The night passed with such pleasant conversation. They shared their Indian meal of rogan josh, chicken tikka and mild vindaloo, wild rice and Bombay potatoes until they couldn't eat another bite. As they finished off the bottle of wine, they made the arrangements for the following day, until eventually Ben stood to go as neither of them could think of another thing to delay his going home.

They walked to the door. Then Liz said suddenly, “You realise your car has been parked outside my house for almost twelve hours? Poor Mrs Mangle won’t have been able to leave her seat all that time in case she missed what time you left.”

“In that case she deserves something very special for her trouble.”

Ben opened the front door as Liz automatically put on the outside light that would illuminate the path but also the two figures at the door. It was at this point that Ben deliberately put his arms around Liz, tilted her head up towards him with his thumb then kissed her long and slowly for what seemed an age. Liz knew she should pull away but she simply couldn’t bring herself to draw back. Her heart stood still. In fact everything about these precious moments seemed to be in slow motion.

Ben was warm and smelled of Indian spices, wood smoke and Armani body spray, and Liz couldn’t think of a nicer fragrance on a man. His lips began to pull away from Liz’s and he took a long slow intake of breath that Liz hoped was his sample of her scent.

"Wow, erm, poor Mrs Mangle will never sleep tonight and it's far too late to put it on the jungle telephone tonight. You're a little bit cruel, do you know that?"

"Well, I'm sorry for Mrs Mangle and her recipients. However, I'm very satisfied. At this precise moment life could not get any sweeter and, on that note, I'd better be off. I'll collect you tomorrow around ten – is that okay?"

She said yes, but just before he walked away he leaned in and gave her a fleeting peck on her lips, saying bye as he did.

Liz had no idea how she was going to sleep tonight, never mind Mrs Mangle. Feeling that she certainly wouldn't sleep, Liz decided to take Barnie for his walk on the common and while walking she had an idea.

Chapter 27

As she was wide awake and would not sleep for hours, Liz decided to prepare for tomorrow's outing with Ben. She knew without being told that he would insist on taking Barnie. The very idea horrified Liz so she hunted in the cupboard for her picnic basket and waterproof blanket, which she would place in the back of the Range Rover for Barnie, regardless of Ben's protestations. She put a chicken in to cook in one of the Aga ovens and in the other she placed some frozen sausage rolls. She would also dig out her large flask and fill it with soup so they had something piping hot to go with the chicken sandwiches and cold sausage rolls. Suitably tired, she went off to bed.

However, Liz should have known she wouldn't find sleep any easier just because she had filled in a couple of hours. She tossed and turned, trying to examine and re-examine the feel of his mouth on hers, the taste of his kisses. Part of her wanted to rewind the part where they were stood at the door but, just as her mind began to replay it and her tongue touched her own lips, the memory disappeared like a puff of smoke. Eventually she must have fallen asleep with exhaustion, until luckily her alarm woke her up. Jumping out of bed with a start, Liz remembered she wasn't going to work today, she was off for a wonderful day out with Ben.

Liz quickly showered then made up the picnic basket and flask and was all ready, complete with waterproof blanket, when he arrived. She wouldn't take any argument about covering the inside of Ben's lovely new Range Rover before Barnie, who Ben had insisted came with them, got in.

"You must be mad, you know, in this lovely car. You do realise he will race around the castle like a mad horse, get soaking wet then steam all of the car windows up on the way home. Ugh, wet dog! Don't say I didn't warn you."

"He's great. To be honest, now that I am going to be at home more than I will be away, I seriously intend to have a dog. I don't want a little dog, either, I want a proper dog, something like a border collie or a golden Labrador. What do you think?"

"I think it's a good idea in principle, but do you realise that every time you go out for the day, you have to remember that you have left a living, breathing, effluent-producing animal in your lovely home with your lovely carpets et cetera. Also you have to remember that even when the weather is tossing down with rain or bleaching down with snow, you must still take doggy out for his or her walk. *They* don't actually care if it rains or snows – they just want to have a good sniff around for their opposite sex.

"You must always remember when choosing your pooch that unless you're fit, or really and truly want to get fit, then a border collie is a working dog and will always be one. However, although greyhounds run for a living they don't actually need that much exercise and make excellent house dogs. I could go on and on but I don't want to put you off and personally I love dogs."

"Well, thank you for that advice, and when I decide to buy my dog I will come to you for your fount of knowledge. And I hope you didn't go to a lot of trouble, as I see you have brought a picnic hamper."

"Well, not exactly a hamper, but I have made us a picnic. I thought that as it's such nice weather but bitter cold we would be better off eating in the warmth of the car as opposed to al fresco."

"You must have been up very early to prepare such a feast, or in bed very late?"

Liz wondered if he was hinting to see if she had prepared it last night, being unable to sleep also.

They arrived at the castle. This time Liz had remembered how she was expected to dress and had worn her heavy duffle coat, not her old one that she used for work but a slightly smarter grey one with bone toggles. She'd known he would insist she wear the bright-coloured hard hat so she had decided on a black sweater and trousers under her grey coat so she didn't look quite as much like an oompaloompa this time.

Ben let Barnie out of the car, who, after creaking to the ground like an old man, suddenly took to his heels and flew round and round the castle grounds. Ben couldn't believe how fast he could run once he got his legs warmed up even at his age and he was becoming quite old for such a large dog, known not to have long lives.

It was a wonderful day – the kind that was so cold it took your breath away but fresh and a pleasure to be outside in. Although it was equally nice to be warmed up inside the car with a hot mug of soup after Ben had almost completed his measurements. When they had finished eating and the dusk was beginning to draw in, Ben said that he needed to takes some photos and that, to give the castle scale. he would like Liz to stand against various walls and window arches while he snapped away with his very expensive digital camera.

Liz wasn't to know that Ben took some rather nice pictures of Liz simply because he wanted to, regardless of the benefits of the architecture. Her little elfin face was all pink and rosy with the bitter cold but you could see the happiness radiating from every smile. She tried to get to his pictures to see what she looked like, saying she didn't want his client to see an oompaloompa on their planned country seat pictures, but Ben moved the ones of her on quickly, saying they were absolutely fine and the client would indeed like them.

Barnie eventually wore himself out and lay in the back of the Range Rover while Liz and Ben took a last walk around the castle just as the dusk was indeed falling and the winter sun had long gone down. Ben took hold of Liz's hand and pulled it through his arm, which at first Liz felt very conscious of, but she soon began to draw closer towards him as she felt the warmth and comfort of his solid frame.

They didn't stop on the way back but made their way home in the darkness in contented silence. Arriving back at Liz's cottage, Ben saw her to the door with Barnie and her empty picnic basket, which they piled into the porch. As she turned to say goodnight he kissed her softly on her half-open, willing lips. With one arm leaning on the frame of the porch, he placed the other around Liz's waist and looked into her face and said, "Thank you, Lizy, for a lovely day, but I better let you go. You have to rehearse for your little bit of espionage tomorrow, if you're sure you won't let me help you?"

"No, no, it'll be nothing, honestly. I'll tell you all about it if you're at the Duck on Tuesday? And thank you for a lovely day too. I've enjoyed myself so much and so has Barnie, although I think you should clean your car out or you will never get rid of the smell of dog, ha ha. And, by the way, we are being watched; I have just seen a curtain twitch and the light go out, a sure sign she is peeking through the curtain now."

"Well, then, I will make her night once again."

He leant down under the lamp and gave Liz a lingering kiss before he walked away and off into the night in his gently purring car.

Chapter 28

Liz picked the phone up from the beside table half asleep, still thinking it must be her alarm clock, only to hear Angus's voice asking if she was sure she didn't need any help.

"No, Angus, I'll be fine, Angus. Yes, Angus, I promise I'll let you know if there's a problem. Bye, Angus, I'll call you later this evening. I promise, Angus."

Then just as she was about to muster up the energy to get out of bed, the phone rang again.

"Yes, Isabel, it's today. No, Isabel, I don't need any help. Yes, I'm sure. I know you would, Isabel, but I can manage, I promise. I will ring you later, yes, I promise. Bye, Isabel."

Liz decided she may as well get up even though her alarm hadn't yet gone off as it was quite clear that she would not get back to sleep. Jumping into the shower she had no sooner climbed out again with a towel wrapped around her when the phone rang again. Still dripping, she clambered to the phone and sighed, saying to the caller, "Yes? Oh, sorry, Ben, no. Well, yes, actually, I'm just getting out of the shower, and yes, it is a bit cold, and yes, I am a bit late. There is a reason for that, though –the phone has not stopped ringing since six thirty a.m., with people asking if I need help. No. It's very kind of you, but I'll manage, honestly, it's not a big job. But thank you anyway. Yes, I'll see you in the Duck tomorrow night if you can make it? Okay, bye then."

Liz arrived at the Mill and parked directly outside Mrs Monroe's flat in the little car park at the front. She unpacked her paint tins and dust sheets in which she had wrapped the camcorder so as not to be seen. She kicked the doors of the van shut noisily and made her way to the main entrance. Just as she entered, as luck would have it, Mrs

Monroe came out of her door as though by coincidence.

"Hello, Mrs Cassidy, I thought you had finished in the Mill until after Christmas?"

"Well, I had, but Angus – you know, Iona's son, we play in the band together – he asked me if I could give his mother's kitchen a quick makeover for Christmas. To tell you the truth, he's a little worried about her. He says he thinks she is going a little senile."

"Oh dear, poor old soul. In what way does he mean?"

"Well, the usual, really. She keeps losing things, you know, her keys, purse, and tablets. Do you know how many times Angus has had to nip over to McLeish and ask for a new prescription? God knows what she does with them; he says she must be flushing them down the loo or something. He's asked me to call at McLeish's today as he'll have a month's supply for her and I've to put them in the kitchen cupboard for her because with Christmas coming he doesn't want her to run out. It's such a shame – she seems as bright as a button. You'd never have thought it, would you? Anyway, merry Christmas to you if I don't see you until afterwards. I'd better get on. Bye."

When Liz arrived at Iona's she could hardly contain herself.

"You will not believe how lucky I was – I've just bumped into Mrs Monroe herself! It was so easy – the conversation automatically came around to the fact that you are going a bit senile and we are having to put extra tablets in the kitchen cabinet in case you run out over the holidays. How perfect is that?"

Liz and Iona went into the kitchen in search of a good place to hide the camera when Liz spotted the perfect place. Iona had an artificial ivy plant in a strange-looking knitted plant holder that hung from the ceiling on the opposite side to the wall cabinets. It was held by a pretty strong-looking brass cup hook and certainly looked as though it would hold the weight of the camcorder.

“Perfect. Iona, do you mind if I put our trap in your plant?”

“Not in the least, my dear, you help yourself. You’ve no need to ask – remember I’m a bit do-lally!”

Liz climbed the little step stool that Iona used to clean her windows, which meant she wouldn’t have any difficulty getting to the camera to turn it on and off. She placed the camera under the bushy ivy plant, making sure that the lens wouldn’t be seen but wasn’t covered. She reminded Iona that she only needed to turn it on when she wasn’t going to be in the room, such as when she went to bed or into the shower. Reminding her that Angus would check it each time he came, Liz told her that hopefully it wouldn’t take long to catch their thief.

After having a coffee with Iona, Liz felt reassured that Iona wasn’t in the least worried about the camera. In fact she was totally animated about the 'catchy monkey', as she referred to Mrs Monroe. Liz left for her cottage.

Driving home, she had to laugh at the way Iona had taken to the little scheme. Old people never ceased to amaze Liz. Anyone who thought elderly people had nothing left to give society hadn't spent any time with them. In actual fact they had more experience, more courage and more common sense than anyone she knew.

Chapter 29

After Liz arrived home it could have been no more than two minutes before Isabel came knocking at the door, all excited to know the ins and outs of the deed.

"Good grief, can a person not get in before I'm interrogated? Actually it couldn't have gone sweeter."

Liz explained how she had made such a noise going into the Mill that Mrs Monroe couldn't have failed to notice her entrance. Iona had done the rest by spreading the word, inadvertently, apparently, that she was coming to decorate her kitchen for her. After Liz had filled Isabel in on all the details, it was her turn to interrogate Isabel.

"Never mind my business, what gives with you and Angus?"

"Oh, Liz, he's the most gentle giant. He is kind and affectionate and I think I'm happier than I have ever been. I have no idea how I never noticed him in that way before. And what about you? A little bird told me you went out early with a certain man in a certain Range Rover with a picnic basket?"

"My God, I don't believe it, you heard that already? Of course, the source would be Mrs Mangle, but how did it get to you so fast?"

"Ha ha, so it's true then?"

"Of course it's true; when has she ever been wrong? I suppose she told your source about the parting at the door?"

"Ohh yesss, we heard all about the long, drawn out kisses under the outside light. Well, you should have known, girl, if you will snog under the lamp the whole village will know by morning. So tell me all."

"Not until you tell me where you heard it from so I know how far it's travelled."

"I heard it from the village shop, and I think it was fresh then, because I actually followed Mrs Mangle into the shop so she must have just passed it on. By the time I was told they weren't saying he had stayed the night, but that his Range Rover was parked there for a very, very long time."

"Ohh, God, my reputation will be in shreds now. Well, to be honest, it was worth every single bit of tittle-tattle. He's really nice, Isabel, he likes dogs, and he even let Barnie into his lovely new car. In fact, he insisted we take him. He likes music, he has a great sense of humour, he loves Indian food and he didn't insist we eat at the table in the kitchen – we ate by the fireside and we chatted about everything and anything and before we knew it…"

"Yes, yes, before you knew it what?"

"Nothing, nosey. Suffice to say, he is a lovely kisser and that's all you're getting to know. For all I know, he may be a serial collector of women. I mean he has Fiona already, so… We've had a lovely couple of outings to a castle that he has been commissioned to work on, an Indian takeaway and a couple of 'rather nice' kisses. But he is a free agent and, come to think of it, so am I and that's that."

The next person to ring up and find out how the mission went was Angus, so it was easier to pass Isabel on to him and let her explain while Liz made the coffee. It was rather strange to hear Isabel's voice soften when speaking to Angus. Rather nice, though, that her two best friends had got together out of the blue.

When Isabel eventually put the phone down, looking at it longingly, Liz commented, "You've really got it bad this time; I don't think I've ever seen you like this before."

The phone rang again instantly, and Isabel answered it, giving that mischievous look she always gave when she intended to tease Liz. "It's Tom for you," she said, handing the phone to Liz.

"Hi, darling, what's up? Are you still coming on Friday with a pile of washing for me as a Christmas present?"

“Well, thank you, darling, if that’s an invite then I’ll definitely take you up on it; although there is no need for you to do my laundry, I’m a big boy now.”

“Oh, oh, I’m sorry. Isabel said it was Tom.” Liz gave Isabel that ‘I’ll kill you’ look while trying not to go all pink until she had put the phone down. She also tried not to think of how he had said the word ‘darling’.

“Hi, sorry, oh, yes, it all went fine. Yes, it’s hidden and Iona played her part beautifully, in fact like an old pro, as they say. These old dears worry me slightly – between my mother and the old gals at the Mill they could teach us young’uns a thing or two, I bet. Yes, I’ll see you at the Duck tomorrow night then. Bye then.”

“Hey, I do believe you’ve got the hots for this guy? Liz, I haven’t seen you blush like that since you and Bob used to make those married type innuendos to each other and make us single folk envy you rotten.”

"Oh, pish… He's a nice guy, I said so, but he has other fish to fry. I'm just the only person he's met in the village and we seem to get on, that's all. Now don't go making a mountain out of a molehill like you normally do, or you might embarrass the poor man."

Chapter 30

After a major conflab with Angus and Isabel about how Liz had hidden the camera, the group unpacked their instruments, then they began to play. They started the night in high spirits with the old age Irish tune, ‘Lord of the Dance’. Then on to ‘Whiskey in the Jar’ and one or two more very lively tunes in order to give the audience the sing-song they loved and expected.

As they sat for a few minutes enjoying a long overdue cold drink and a chat among themselves, Liz noticed Ben arrive. Without warning he took up her bodhrán, which was on the seat next to her in the hope that he would come. Then suddenly the mournful sounds of a tin whistle could be heard somewhere outside and coming closer, playing a tune that would have made the hair stand up on the back of anyone’s neck, ‘Local Hero’, and Liz knew it was Tom.

As he came closer into the room and took his place next to Liz, Ben began a very slow and quiet tapping of the bodhrán, keeping time with the mournful song. Then one by one the other players joined in with the haunting Mark Knopfler lyrics made famous in the film of the same name, *Local Hero*. From the audience came a steady mmm, mmm, mmmmmmm, until eventually everyone in the room was humming to the haunting sound, which then erupted in a roar of applause.

It was obvious to the audience that there would be a momentary break while the band greeted Tom, whom many knew to be Liz's son, obviously home for the Christmas holidays.

Tom lifted his mother from her perch where Angus had placed her and gave her a bear hug of a greeting and she became swallowed up before she could kiss him in turn.

Ben was beside her. Liz was really pleased to see him and to know he had come after all, as when she had arrived at the Duck and his Range Rover was nowhere to be seen she had thought he wasn't coming. She suddenly came out of her reverie and began the introduction of Ben to Tom.

"Tom, I would like you to meet Ben, he's…"

"Yes, we've met. He's the rich dude from the big house, who just helped me mend my puncture outside his place, in his clean duds as well."

"You've got that wrong, Tom. You and all the people in this village are the rich ones – I would just like to join in."

"We seem as though we are permanently indebted to you where vehicles are concerned, Mr Paris," Liz said in a mock eighteenth-century manner. "I thank you on behalf of my son, and me, once again."

Then Liz said more casually, "I had thought maybe you weren't coming for some reason?"

“Wasn’t coming? I wouldn’t have missed this for the world. You really know how to bring a lump to the throat with your choice of music. And what a wonderful rendition, Tom, from the tin whistle. Who would have ever thought such a haunting sound could come from such a simple instrument. You make me wish more than anything that I had been taught to play a proper musical instrument.”

“You play the bodhrán; you have a feel for the beat, I can tell. You simply need to be shown. Anyone can play an instrument – it just takes practice, and the desire to play, of course. It helps if your mum and dad are musicians because you don’t feel such a sissy, of course, being a boy.”

Liz watched as the two men talked easily, before Angus hugged Tom in a gruff manly way and said it was good to see him, but shouldn’t they get back to the music of the night. Everyone agreed. Tom did have one request, though, which was that, as it was Christmas, they played The Pogues’ ‘Fairytale of New York’, the one with Kirsty

McColl. Everybody knew the tune, although it turned out that Liz would have to do the main singing part, which was more or less a solo, with the rest of it taken by the guys. Complaining a little, Liz said that she wasn't a solo singer but she would do her best.

The whole of the Duck sang along and in the end they had to do several choruses of the song before going on to the next. It was soon time for 'The Wild Rover', signalling the end of the evening and the usual uplifting of spirits that made even the most melancholy person contented.

As the band packed away their instruments, Tom caught each person's eye that passed, returning their greeting and giving his best of the season to them all. Then he announced he was starving and he thought they should all collect fish and chips on the way home and eat them in front of the fire.

"And that includes you, Ben, unless you're in a hurry to get back to your posh house, of course?"

"Tom! Er, sorry, Ben, please excuse my son, he has a student's turn of phrase, but what he says he means kindly and so do I. You're more than welcome?"

"Are you sure? Won't you be wanting to catch up with all his news from uni? He has only just got back."

"Take my word for it, we'll have plenty of time to catch up and we are very, very grateful for your helping him with his flat tyre, especially when you were all dressed to come out. You are a knight of the road, and I doff my hat to you, sir." Liz made the gesture of doffing her hat and they walked happily towards their cars, which they drove in convoy towards Liz's little cottage. Tom had been given the job of collecting the fish and chips while Liz and Ben built the fire up and made everything ready. Isabel and Angus got the glasses out and poured the wine, which Liz admitted was more plonk than posh but it would go well with fish and chips.

They all sat around the fire, eating fish and chips, and drinking cheap wine, which tasted like nectar when in good company. They all chatted easily and the laughter flowed like the wine. Liz looked from Tom to Ben and she could see how easily they chatted, about literature, colleges, Edinburgh and different student haunts that they both recognised. She didn't know why, but she was glad that they appeared to be getting on well.

When the talk came around to the drugs and the hidden camera, Liz attempted to shake her head in Tom's directions, trying frantically to indicate to them to hush. However, Isabel and Angus were in full flow and thought Liz was simply being modest. Until Tom stopped them, asking, "What drugs?"

"Uh-oh," said Isabel as she looked from Liz to Angus and pulled a face. She had thought Liz would have told Tom all about it.

"What about drugs, Mum? What are they talking about?"

"It's nothing, Tom, and don't think for one moment that I was in any danger, because I wasn't."

"Danger? Danger? That makes it worse. Tell me, for goodness sake."

Ben went to speak, presumably to help Liz out, so Liz began to explain herself. She told Tom how the drugs had been going missing and how they had all decided to do something about it, including his grandmother. Liz added that she was sure it had been her mother's suggestion in the first place to use a camera.

"But I can assure you there was never at any time any danger. So are we okay with that? I never thought I would be explaining my life to my nineteen-year-old son – the other way around would be more natural."

"Sorry, Mum, yes, it's all right now, I'll let you off. But, Mum, you should have told me."

“Why? What good would that have done? You would have just warned me off. Your grandma thought it was a brilliant plan.”

“Ha ha, she would. She’s a tough old bird, isn’t she?” he said rhetorically and Liz laughed, asking why it was all right for his grandmother to do things but not his mother. To which Tom grabbed a hold of his mother and lifted her up as easily as a soft toy.

“That’s why. You’re not as big as two penn’orth of copper. What do you think, Ben?”

“I have to agree. The first time I met your mother I thought she was the decorator’s apprentice. But hey, don’t worry, your mum has guts, and she wasn’t alone. We – Angus, Isabel and I – were all with your mum, well, technically speaking, we were on the end of the phone. And there really wasn’t any danger or I wouldn’t have let her go alone.”

“Ohhwa!” Isabel said in her usual, knowing way, which hinted at all kinds of innuendos. And which insinuated that Ben’s relationship with Liz was closer than mere friendship alone. Liz actually quite liked the fact that it sounded as though Ben felt protective towards her. It had been a long time since she had felt protected, and it was nice.

"Well, that's all right, as long as I know that she has you for back-up, Ben, then I won't worry so much. I was worried for a while that that prat Niiigel was making moves on Mum. I thought I'd come home some half term and he would have moved in. Yuck, what a creep."

"Tom, that's not fair. Nigel meant well and he could be very kind."

"Liz, the consensus of opinion is that the man is a prat and was only after you for your organisational skills, free labour and your rather nice cottage, which he would have expected you to keep in good decorative order. I wonder if he ever actually noticed you were a woman."

"Amen to that, Isabel," said Angus, who felt he could agree now that the can of worms was open and he was allowed his say at last. "The man was blind as a bat – he never saw you as a kind-hearted, beautiful, talented woman. He saw you as a meal ticket. And another thing – anyone who doesn't like music, well, they're not our sort of people at all."

"Well said, Angus. I have no idea how I've managed to get through my life without knowing how much pleasure could be had by listening to such wonderful sounds as folk music. Each song seems to evoke such feelings of pure happiness, sadness and melancholy, that you cannot help but be immersed in it, and each and everyone of your audience takes that warm feeling home with them," Ben said, feeling slightly embarrassed at making such a speech, however much he meant it.

"Well, it makes me feel good, anyway."

"It should make you feel good, I think. That's what music is for – to chase away the blues, to cheer you up, to make you want to dance or join in. It's a coming together of communities in song, as Bob used to say. Do you remember, Tom? He loved it when the whole pub sang along; he said it made it all worthwhile, and you're right, that's how music should make you feel, like it's to be shared by all."

"What instrument would you like to play, Ben, if you could learn?" Tom said.

"Well, do you know, I think I'll try to perfect the bodhrán. I love the sound and I do think I have some rhythm as well. Secretly, though, well, I loved the sound of the tin whistle. Is it very hard to learn?"

"No, no, really it isn't, and I have a feeling we are going to be seeing a lot of you so when I'm home I wouldn't mind giving you a few lessons."

"Do you know I'm going to take you up on that? I'll get myself a whistle and a beginner's book and practise in my office where nobody will hear the din. I'm determined to learn."

As the impromptu party broke up with mentions of work in the morning and so forth, Isabel and Angus kissed Liz saying their goodnights and off they went, at which point Ben said he would also go and allow Liz some time with Tom.

"Thank you, both, I've really enjoyed my night once again and it was a pleasure to meet you, Tom. I think you are a credit to your parents. Oh, by the way, Liz, I'm busy working on the plans for the new hall. I wonder, if anything arises, can I contact you, rather than Nigel, as I'm sure you actually put together the questionnaire in the first place?"

"That sounds like Mum. Catch ya later, Ben, nice meeting you and thanks again for the rescue," Tom said openly, as he made moves to go inside. That would give his mother time to say goodnight to Ben, as it was fairly obvious to anyone's eyes that there was something going on between the two of them, even if they didn't recognise it.

Liz suddenly felt a little tongue-tied as it was fairly obvious the way everyone had ceremoniously left that they were 'giving them space', as it were, which made Liz feel a little awkward. However, Ben seemed unaffected by their tactful retreat, saying, "You have a lovely family and really good friends, that's a very rare thing in the city. I envy you, Liz, very much. I meant it when I said I would love to be part of it. I would like to know you well enough to stop having to find excuses to see you!"

Ben had spoken with a query in his eye, awaiting Liz's answer with baited breath in case he saw the kind of look born out of good manners. He needn't have worried as he hardly dared expect the look that was quite obvious and sincere in Liz's deep brown eyes.

"You have my permission not to have to find a reason to call on me or ring me. You are more than welcome and I'm sure Tom feels exactly the same. You two seem to have got off to a really good start, which is more than he ever did or ever would with Nigel."

"Ha ha, men and motors, you know, and it's amazing what you find to talk about while crawling around in the dark changing a tyre. Once we realised we had you in common, well, there was no stopping us. Tom chatted about you and even about his dad. He misses him to talk to quite a lot, I think, but he thinks you're terrific, did you know that?"

"Yeah, we're good friends. I suppose we're closer since Bob died but then we always were a close family. Even though my mum is miles away in Benidorm, she knows everything that's happening in the village, and she is also a remarkable woman. Anyway, listen, don't be a stranger, and if I don't see you before, I'll see you at the pantomime on Saturday night."

"Oh, will you not be at the Duck on Thursday night?"

"No. Oh, I forgot to say, the Duck has lots of Christmas meals in the run-up to Christmas, parties and stuff, so we don't meet on the last Thursday. But don't forget what I told you – call in any time."

Ben leant down and kissed Liz warmly but all too fleetingly on her lips then, as he walked towards the gate, he turned, saying, "I may just do that, good Lizy."

Liz watched Ben's car drive away, and as she walked back into the kitchen she realised that Tom had been standing leaning against the door frame and he had a huge smile on his face.

"I wasn't listening, honest. I had finished washing the dishes and was about to ask if we should take Barnie for a midnight walk?"

"Yes, we should. That's exactly what I would like to do with my son. Give me two minutes to get my boots and coat on."

They walked arm in arm on the common. It was a beautiful moonlit night and the sky was full of stars twinkling millions of light years away.

“So how’s life for you, Tom? Is there a girlfriend in the offing? I mean, someone a little more serious than a first date.”

“Mum, you know me, I’m not a one-night stand, I respect myself,” Tom said, just like his father in his best stuffed shirt imitation, which made them both giggle together.

“And what about you, Mum? Is there someone new in your life? Hmm, eh, hmm? Called Ben, maybe?”

“Tom, he is a friend. A new friend, yes, and how it happened exactly I don’t actually know. After all he was a client whom I worked for but somehow we seem to keep bumping into each other and well… Yes, I do enjoy his company. But before you start running away with that, he has a partner, Fiona, in Edinburgh.”

“You mean partner in business or partner in love?” Tom said in his own inimitable way.

“Well, to be honest, I don’t know. He goes to Edinburgh on business sometimes and she comes here and, er, stays over so I don’t know and that’s the truth. Now, can we leave Ben alone?”

“Well, I can, but I think you’re stuck on him. And you know, Mum, in case you were wondering, I think it’s time you had a friend, a man friend to share the rest of your life with. You’re a great person, you know, and I’ll always have you, but you need someone too. Just as long as it’s not…”

“Niiigel” they both said in unison, and then laughed, a wonderful sound that rang out into the darkness as Barnie tore around the field all on his own.

Chapter 31

Wednesday morning Liz had a sudden urge to nip into town and buy a small present for Ben. She had decided that she couldn't possibly let him stay alone in that huge house on Christmas. She also had to go to a main post office to send her annual parcel to her mother for Christmas, which consisted of all the things she couldn't buy over there – just the luxuries, because certain things were now universal, of course.

She decided on a warm scarf for Ben as she was sure he probably bought his clothes from some very exclusive Edinburgh boutique, but a scarf in Juniper Green in the winter never came in wrong and it was just a little something to put under the tree for him.

On her way back she suddenly decided she would call and see the village hall plans. Ben had, after all, asked her. As she drove her little van up the drive she suddenly realised it had been a bad idea as who should she see coming out of the house? Fiona. She slammed the door as though she were in a really bad temper. However, Liz thought to herself, she would look a bit silly if she simply turned around and left. So she mustered up as much height as she could and began a pleasant hello. Fiona suddenly let off a barrage of obvious dislike for the fact that Liz was there, actually on Ben's drive, let alone his home.

"You do realise he has a dicky heart or something? It would be such a pity to have two men die on you, you being so young and all."

And with that Fiona stormed over to her car and drove off in a hail of gravel. Liz had absolutely no idea what on earth she had meant, and why was she so angry with her? One look around the drive and the corner of the house brought her attention to the fact that Ben's Range Rover wasn't there so he quite obviously wasn't home, yet Fiona had come out of the house. Did that mean she had been sleeping overnight?

Liz turned the van around as fast as she could and drove off down the road as though the devil himself was after her. For some reason she didn't want Ben to see her and know that she knew Fiona and him had been together, and that for whatever reason Fiona had spat out those awful words of venom at her.

When she arrived back home Tom had left a note to say he had gone to the garage to have his spare tyre mended and do a little bit of Christmas shopping and he would see her later. Liz decided to take Barnie on to the common so she could have a good think. Good old Barnie, he was better than any therapist.

Liz walked and talked to herself as she went. Why would Fiona say a thing like that? Why would she want her to know that Ben had a bad heart? If he did have a bad heart. But if he had, why did she feel she had to warn Liz off? Was it because she was jealous of her? Liz gave herself a little self-indulgent chuckle.

Well, maybe she is, we do get on very well. Liz continued talking away to herself. But, on the other hand, why does she seem to keep coming out of his house? Is she sleeping with him? Are they a couple or simply work colleagues? Oh, I don't know, she exasperated. On the other hand, she carried on, not to be put off. Why tell me? He did say when he arrived at the village that he wanted to change his lifestyle and that was why he had bought the house. Also he has told me on numerous occasions he wants less work and only the work he finds challenging and not the bread and butter work, so he is definitely cutting down his work load. Supposing, just supposing, I did fall for him. I said supposing. Oh, who am I kidding? The reason I'm having this soul-searching conversation is because I have fallen for him, hook, line and sinker. And how would I feel if he has got a problem with his heart? How ill is he? I couldn't bear to lose another person I love, I couldn't bear to go through it all over again, Liz told herself with a deep sob in her voice. She walked in silence with all kinds of thoughts of Bob running through her head, of the happy times, of the sad times when he was going through his chemo treatment and was weak and sick. Yet they could still talk and be with each other. They still gave each other comfort and they always had Tom. Bob would say don't be a coward – if you love him, for however long, give it a shot. He was right, she wasn't a coward, but oh God, if she let herself fall deeply in love and the worst happened, could she take it all over again?

Barnie had long since got tired and was now meekly walking beside Liz as she carried on her inner turmoil of what-ifs. She thought about Isabel and Angus being a couple, and she thought about her mother feeling the loss of two people who, no matter how nice, were simply friends, yet her mother felt their loss and feelings of loneliness that she could hear in her mother's voice. Did she want to be lonely in the hope that one day she would find some perfect guy who could promise not to die? Of course not, so what then?

What are you telling yourself, you silly woman?

"To take what you can while you can, and grab it with both hands and hang on tight. No matter how short the time, enjoy every moment. Yes. Yes. Yes. Come on, Barnie, we're going home now."

Liz decided she would bake. She would bake and bake and invite all her favourite friends on Christmas Eve. Like her and Bob used to in the old days, before illness had forced a calmness to inhabit the house, owing to his treatment. She would invite the group and tell them to bring their instruments. They all tended to be single men and alone, which is what Bob used to say.

"You don't want them to be alone on Christmas Eve, now, do you?"

She would ring them up and tell them, she would let Isabel and Angus know, and she would ring Ben herself later when she had finished baking. To hell with Fiona. She would take her chances, no matter how short the time, and she decided if he had any interest in her whatsoever then she would reciprocate right back.

As she had no idea when Tom would arrive home, and having baked until she could have happily dropped, she decided that takeaway was on the menu again. Good old takeaways, what did we do before them?

The front door slammed at approximately seven thirty as Tom's door shutting almost stopped the clock with the force so you couldn't fail to notice.

"Hi, Mum, sorry I'm late. You'll never guess where I've been? And what I've been doing?"

All this was said while Tom called out from the bathroom, so that by the time he had come down the stairs Liz was agog with curiosity.

"So where have you been? And what have you been doing that I won't ever guess?"

“Guess whose Range Rover I followed back halfway from Edinburgh to the village?”

Liz felt a little flush of excitement and attempted to hide her interest although she couldn’t wait to hear all about it.

“Ben’s, of course, you ninny,” Tom said when he had no forthcoming answer to his quizzical request. “I thought, first of all, who on earth is that mad fool, with such a massive tree tied to the roof rack of such a lovely car? Then as soon as he turned towards the village I knew who it was. Then when he pulled into his drive I thought I’d go in and have a wee keek.

“Well, there was no way he was going to be able to get that down off the roof without damaging his car and then inside the house. So I returned the favour I owed him and helped him inside with it. Then it was a two-man job just to get the thing to stand up. It’s a good job I’m a big strong laddie. Anyway we managed it and as a thank you he showed me around his fabulous house. I’ll tell you what, Mum, he sang your praises all the way round the house. He pointed out all the work you did for him and how he thought you were an expert. He showed me his office – wow, what a fantastic room, and erm… Well, he talked about you an awful lot."

It was a strange thing. Liz was sure Tom had been going to tell her something then had changed his mind. And she was greedy for information as to what Ben had said to him about her, like a teenage girl about a boy she liked.

"Oh, and, by the way, I've invited him to come over on Christmas Eve. I told him we always have folk at our house. He agreed as long as we agree to go to his house on New Year's Eve so I said yeah that would be great, okay?"

"Okay, well you seem to have covered more or less everything I was going to do."

"He's going to Edinburgh tomorrow, I gather. He says he's in the middle of tying things up with the division of the company or something like that."

"What did he say he was doing, Tom?"

"Well, to be honest, Mum, I was so busy looking round the house and chatting about Edinburgh and how he loved it when he was my age but now finds it exhausting. We chatted about different bars and restaurants and stuff, which he says he doesn't miss at all any more. He says he prefers the company of the people in Juniper Green. I think he meant one in particular…"

Liz was extremely curious, to say the least, but didn't want to sound as though she was more interested than anyone else would be about Ben Paris's movements.

Chapter 32

Saturday dawned and the day of the pantomimes had arrived. The children's nativity would be on from two o'clock until four. This was basically attended by the proud parents of those involved and some of the residents from the Mill. Angus and Isabel had kindly offered to take half a dozen of the residents. They would use two cars, which allowed plenty of room as some of the older ones were not terribly flexible and one or two needed walking frames.

Angus was an absolute treasure and was as gentle and caring with each as he was with his own mother. The evening performance, which was *Cinderella*, started at seven and finished roughly at nine o'clock. This was usually attended by a much younger crowd that included some of the young farmers who had bit parts, so great hilarity ensued from their many friends and families in the audience. Thank goodness, Nigel had had nothing to do with the actual content of the productions, or he would have soon stamped out any frivolity. His role was always organisational, and he took it very seriously indeed.

Tom and Liz were enjoying some lazing around time before dressing for the pantomime that evening when there was a phone call that they would always remember.

"BINGO!" the excited voice of Angus boomed down the phone.

"Voilà, she took the bait. She must have known the whole building would be more or less empty while all the oldies were at the panto. And for some reason I thought, after dropping mother off, I'll check the camcorder… And there she was in all her glory, as clear as day! Oh, you have no idea how thrilled I was to see it. I've watched it over and over and over again. Listen, I'll call over now and bring it to you to show you, then I think it should go straight to the police while the trail is hot. What do you think? Or whatever – we'll discuss it when I get there. Oh, I'm absolutely thrilled, you clever, clever, clever girl, you."

"Wow, Mum," said Tom, "no need to tell me, I heard every booming word of it. You are a clever little spy. Mighty mouse, that's you. Brill, Mum, you did this all on your own – and I thought you needed a minder while I was away. Ha ha, that's a joke."

Angus arrived within minutes and they watched the seemingly innocuous act of Mrs Monroe simply walking into the empty flat then entering the kitchen. They saw a glimpse of her and then she went towards the particular cupboard… Voilà, as Angus had said. There she was as clear as clear could be. There was absolutely no doubt that this would convict her for stealing with intent to sell as the quantity could not be argued as being for personal use.

Angus picked Liz up and swung her round and round, saying she was a genius and no one would ever have suspected Mrs Monroe had it not been for her idea of the camera.

"Well, to be fair, it was my mother's idea! She deserves half of the credit. She was the one who suggested we hide a camera. Wait until I tell her – she will be beside herself that she wasn't able to be in on the sting, as she will no doubt put it."

Chapter 33

After they had all arrived at the village hall, Angus and Isabel, Tom and Liz were standing around chatting before the performance. Each of them was still full of self-importance at their part in their little subterfuge. All the while, Liz was keeping an eye out for the familiar, dark floppy hair of Ben, above the others' heads who were arriving. As soon as she saw him she waved him across and he was immediately bombarded with a deep-throated whisper of excited voices passing on the story and the triumph of their plot.

"You clever girl, you. You never cease to amaze me in the things you can achieve. So what now? What's the next stage? Do you take it to the police?"

"Angus has already done that. They have the camcorder at this very moment, " Tom said proudly. "And I thought she needed looking after! Wasn't I underestimating this little bundle? Dad always said she was a holy terror when roused, although I always thought he was joking."

"I think this deserves a celebration and I would like you all, as I have you all together, to come to my home for a joint celebration of New Year's and victory for the little man, but in this case little woman."

There were murmurs of "You're on," and "Sounds great," until they all eventually took their seats inside for the performance of *Cinderella*. It would undoubtedly be a success, as the present group were all geared up to be a noisy and excitable audience before it even started.

It wasn't until they were sat down that Liz realised she had somehow ended up sitting next to Ben, and as the village hall seats were quite small and packed together they were, in fact, very, very close, which was nice, thought Liz. Had she only realised it, Ben also thought the same, especially as he had manoeuvred himself beside her.

The performance was indeed a great success and almost lifted the roof off the old hall. It was then that Ben stood up and walked over to Nigel. After a short discussion with him, Ben walked up on to the stage.

"I would like to say firstly what a wonderful performance of *Cinderella* that was, and to each and every one of the performers a very, very well done. I would also like to thank those behind the scenes or in this case those who make the scenery for these wonderful performances and who often get forgotten. Mrs Liz Cassidy."

There was a general whistling and clapping for Liz who was forced to stand and take a short bob of embarrassment. He went on to read out a list of helpers, which Nigel had obviously given him. It was then that he asked the audience to thank Mr Nigel Finch, the organiser of both the performances of this year's pantomimes. But also for his unstinting time, which he was giving so freely in an effort to provide the village of Juniper Green with a new village hall. He advised that, for those people who were interested, copies of the plans were pinned up in the lobby and could be read and commented on at any time before they became finalised.

Ben went on, "And there is one other thing that Mr Finch doesn't know. A member of the parish council in a neighbouring village has approached me about the plans, which have been tentatively submitted for initial approval. And they are very interested in Mr Finch project managing the building of their village hall, too. As soon as appropriate funds can be found, that is, which is another reason why they need him to be involved as he is now very much qualified to give advice on the subject."

For the first time in Nigel's life a great cheer went up in the village hall for him – just him. Ben indicated for Nigel to come up on to the stage and take a bow, which he did. Liz clapped and looked from Ben to Nigel and thought what a wonderful kind man he was – Ben that is, not Nigel. But she thought how nice it was for Nigel, for the first time in his life, for him to feel he was important.

And that the applause was actually for him. He seemed to grow at least two feet taller.

They buzzed and chatted all the way home and, as nobody had brought their cars, knowing the car park would be packed, they all walked in companionable excitement. Angus and Isabel linked arms, Tom more or less moved between groups, then Liz felt her arm being pulled through the crook of Ben's arm, which felt just right.

"That was a really nice thing you did for Nigel, Ben, he looked so happy and puffed up with self-importance. It will be something he will never forget. And I can't get over the fact that you are going to let him project manage the building of both village halls. Do you have that much faith in his ability?"

"Well, you've said it yourself, when does Nigel do anything himself? He's an organiser, a delegator, and actually there isn't anything wrong with that in business. As long as he doesn't delegate or dump stuff on you then I think it's a great idea. It will keep him busy, off your back, and, to be honest, he did seem to be so happy, which in some ridiculous way I think he deserved. Don't worry, I feel sure my mobile number will be keyed into his speed dial, for when he needs assurance."

"And you won't mind that? I thought you were trying to cut down on your involvements?"

"That is true, but two little village halls are nothing compared to the amount of work I used to take on, on my own. He'll be fine – he will simply need guidance and assurance, that's all. Now that he feels he is so important he will want to do things himself to prove himself."

The group began to inevitably string out and Ben and Liz became the last pair dawdling along at their own pace. Ben looked down to see Liz's face shining in the moonlight and said, "You know, I've never met anyone like you in my entire life. Do you know that? I don't even know anyone who resembles you. In my line of work you meet different types of people and they all fit into sort of groups, if you understand. But you, well, you're unique."

"Well, thank you, kind sir, but actually there are me and Ronnie Corbett in that small group." Liz laughed at her own small joke.

"You know, you're quite special yourself. How nice of you to do that, firstly for the village hall, and then to give the credit to Nigel."

They strolled along a little farther before Ben said, "Do you know, if this is a sample of the happiness I'm going to feel at this moment in time then 'bring it on', as Tom would likely say. If I hadn't been warned to change my life or… Well, I may never have bought Juniper Manor, never met you and your wonderful friends and family. And it was all out there all the time, going about its merry life, without me in it. It's hard to credit."

"Hey, it's not all simply the village, you know. Life is what you bring to it. Tonight,

Nigel got a taste of what it's like if you try, just a little bit, to socialise. He's not used to it, he's used to giving orders, so he didn't realise how much pleasure it is to give or be given. I still think he'll be a pain in the butt. However, I think he now knows what it feels like to be liked. But you've brought a lot to our little village already, and you have opened yourself up to all the new experiences that allow you to socialise. You love the music and the group, you like all my friends, and I even think you get on with my cheeky son."

And me, she had been about to say, when he jumped in saying, "I like you. You and your friends and family are very easy to like – you are all so genuine, you care about each other and the groups is like a… a friendly hug every Tuesday and Thursday, so that even if you feel out of sorts it's worth going just to make you feel better. This is where I would like to make not only my house but my home, too, and wasn't I lucky to have got the best decorator in the village?"

"Ha ha, the only decorator in the village, more to the point. You didn't have a lot of choice."

"Yes, but you came highly recommended. And that reminds me – I must send a thank you for that, I will forever be indebted."

They arrived at Liz's cottage as per usual and for the next hour they made huge inroads into the mince pies and mini quiches Liz had made during her baking frenzy. They all stood up to leave, including Ben, and as everyone was filing out of the door, to Liz's surprise, instead of waiting until everyone had left, Ben leaned over and kissed her in the darkness of the porch. He casually leant down and claimed Liz for all to see with his warm lips. The kiss wasn't the longest they had shared. However, it was a statement to those who witnessed it, which included Tom.

Liz wondered briefly whether that had been Ben's intention – to see how Tom took this obvious closeness towards his mother. Tom seemed to be nothing but happy with the situation, giving his mother his best nudge, nudge, wink, wink look, which everyone clearly saw and laughed at as they left quite noisily, meaning that Mrs Mangle didn't miss a thing.

Chapter 34

Christmas Eve dawned crisp and white. Liz managed to summon Tom out of bed so that they could organise the furniture, which was always pushed back against the walls in order that the group had somewhere to sit while they played. Christmas, it had been decided, wouldn't be complete without music. Bob used to say you could fill the house with the sweet smell of baking and turkey but music fed the soul and rang the season in.

The food was laid out on the large kitchen table and a massive metal ornamental bucket was sat on top of the Aga with delicious-smelling hot soup in it. Then the last of the sausage rolls came out of the oven and on to a long serving plate. Once this was done, Liz decided it was time for her to have a long soak in the tub.

Earlier that day she had placed all her gifts under the tree for her friends, including

Ben's scarf. She had decided that Christmas was eventually sorted. And as she dressed after having had a wonderful long soak, she thought about how she would usually have to put on her wellies and take Barnie out for his last walk of the night. But, for some reason, Tom had told her not to bother – that he would do it. Although Liz normally enjoyed taking Barnie, tonight she wanted to spend a little extra time dressing. She told herself that it wasn't for Ben's benefit, although she knew instantly that it was a big fat lie.

She had decided to wear the beautiful black dress she had bought when she and Isabel had gone shopping. As she slipped the soft, superfine merino wool over her head and smoothed it down over her full bosom, shapely hips and washboard-flat tummy, before turning around to see herself in the old pine cheval mirror, nothing could have prepared her for the shock of seeing herself dressed as a woman, with curves and a femininity she hadn't felt for such a long time that she had almost forgotten what it felt like.

She had a pair of black, patent leather shoes with lovely fancy buckles on the front and small heels, which somehow gave her height without being obvious and also she felt very comfortable in them, she reasoned.

Her hair, as usual, needed nothing but a comb through it and to her eyes she gave a lick of mascara. Then she added a dash of CK1, her favourite perfume, and that was that.

When Isabel and Angus arrived they gave her a low long whistle designed to flatter and please, which of course it did. Isabel was no slouch either – she looked a million dollars in the beautiful plum-coloured soft jersey dress that, when she gave a twirl, flared out beautifully. Angus had obviously already given Isabel his opinion on that as his eyes lit up when he looked at her.

It became an open house as the band began to arrive and coats were dumped in the bedroom and instrument cases filled up the porch. The aroma of hot food permeated the whole house and Christmas Eve officially began. Liz was conscious that as the night went on Tom hadn't got back with Barnie and Ben hadn't arrived, which surprised her as she knew he was really keen to come and join in the fun. However, being not only the host but also the fiddle player, before she knew it she was so busy her mind was completely distracted from her own thoughts.

Suddenly the lights flashed on and off two or three times, which halted the music and the procedures, as everyone thought they were about to start the hunts for candles as a power cut seemed imminent.

Then Tom burst into the room and asked for a drum roll from the bodhrán, which from out of nowhere was being held by a handsomely dressed Ben, who looked rather gorgeous, Liz absent-mindedly thought, in his two shades of deep and light blue shirt and navy trousers. He looked casual but dressed up at the same time.

Ben duly gave a very fine drum roll and Tom played 'We Wish You a Merry Christmas', which everyone joined in with, and suddenly the door from the kitchen opened and in walked…

"Mum, Mum, how… How did you get here?"

"Merry Christmas, my darling, I'm your Christmas gift from Ben."

As Florence and Liz hugged, the music played in the background, while Liz was still absolutely shell shocked.

"How on earth did you get here?"

"By plane, darling, what do you think, I swam all the way? You can thank your gorgeous boyfriend here and my wonderful grandson."

"Well, hang on there," Tom piped up. "This was Ben's idea. He organised the flight and the surprise and everything. All I supplied was the telephone number of Gran's condo."

Liz turned to look at Ben, who said with a slight roll of the eyes and a tilt of the chin, "Merry Christmas, Liz."

And he leaned down in full view of half the village, kissed her and at the same time lifted her off her feet. And as the loud whistling and clapping roared, he whispered in her ear, "You look gorgeous, Mrs Cassidy."

"Why, thank you, Mr Paris, and how will I ever thank you for such a wonderful present as this?"

"Don't worry, I'll think of something. Now go and talk to your mum; we have all the time in the world."

Liz and her mother talked for a few minutes. But they were both so glad to see each other and there was so much to catch up on that they decided a late night would be had and they would catch up properly then. In the meantime she was the fiddle player at a party.

Midnight came and everyone kissed each other merry Christmas then the party began to break up and the coats became fewer as did the instrument cases until eventually they had the house to themselves. The five most important people were left in Liz's life. As they cosied with a quiet drink in their hands, Ben sat with his arm around Liz's shoulders, Isabel and Angus sat almost on top of each other – they had become inseparable – and Tom was almost asleep on the floor with a half-full beer glass still in his hand. Liz gently removed it and he never moved a muscle. Florence relayed her conversation with Liz's new man friend to her daughter, looking at both Liz and Ben for approval. As there was no objection from either she carried on with her tale.

"As soon as Ben said who he was and what he wanted me to do, it was game on."

"Mum, where do you get those expressions?"

"Honey, I watch a lot of television over there. To tell you the truth, there's nothing better to do. There's only so much sunbathing you can do and I've done it. And I'm ready for a new start, so I hope you don't mind but you have a lodger for a while until I can find somewhere more permanent."

"Mum, were you serious about looking after the Mill?"

"Was I? What I wouldn't do to get a place like that and to get paid on top is no one's business. Why? Oh, I forgot to ask, how did the sting go?"

And as tired as they all were, they all burst out laughing. Tom said, "That's exactly what Mum said you would say if you had been in on it."

"You're darn tootin' I would, I gave her the idea to hide the camera. If I had been here I would have hidden it myself. Oh, nothing like that ever happened over there."

"So what do you think? Once the police have dealt with Mrs Monroe, how about we all send a letter to the effect that you were instrumental with Liz in trapping Mrs Monroe and have since thought you would like to take on the challenge of becoming the warden of the Mill?"

"Oh my God, Isabel, Liz, what do you think? I would absolutely love to do it. Do you think they would entertain me? They don't really know me. I haven't exactly worked in that type of industry before."

"Mum," "Gran," "Florence," were all said in unison. They told her how she had been instrumental in catching a criminal and that her daughter not only spent half her working life in that building but was also very, very well known and liked and had also been instrumental by hiding the trap.

"And you wonder if they would have you?" said Angus. "Of course they'll have you. They'll probably up your wages as well as have your flat decorated."

"By the best decorator in Juniper Green?" Florence asked.

Everyone laughed.

“Then I’m your gal. And, Liz, you’ve found a jewel in Ben, I hope you know that. With your work you won’t find many other men with his attributes willing to take someone who wears dungarees all day long.”

“My God, she’s only been back two hours and she’s already trying to marry me off.”

“I must say, for a girl who normally wears the sexiest dungarees, I like you even better in your party dress.” As he said this, Ben lifted his eyes and pulled a face that promised more to come. The presents were opened from beneath the tree. When it came to Ben’s parcel, Liz said she felt a little embarrassed. After all, it was just meant to be a small gift.

“I mean, how on earth do you match delivering your mother by plane to your doorstep?”

“Well, I have one idea, and when you all come to my house on New Year’s Eve, if you look on my Christmas tree, I think you'll find something from me to you."

"But, Ben, you have just given me my Christmas!"

"Yes, and when you open the one on my tree that will be mine, I promise you."

Chapter 35

Christmas seemed to roll over in a muddle of lazy days, where Liz and Florence lazed about catching up, making plans and eating and drinking together. Having her mother and Tom in her home made Liz almost feel like the Christmases of the past, only without the one ingredient that used to bind them all together – Bob. But Liz felt that where there had always been a vast void that she had thought could never be filled after Bob died, suddenly it was gone and she didn't feel that any more. She felt hope, warmth, comfort, friendship, but she also felt a glimmer of doubt. Was there more to Ben that she didn't know?

Liz knew one thing clearly after speaking to her mother, a wise old bird as she herself put it. She knew she must ask Ben straight out – how exactly did he and Fiona figure? [her mother's words] and he must come clean about the state of his heart [also her mother's quaint, eloquently put phrase].

The remainder of the Christmas holidays were taken up with the practicalities of the police report about the drugs and Mrs Monroe and her son's involvement. Liz relayed information she had got off some of the ladies in the building about the fact that Mrs Monroe's wayward son had been seen not only by them but also by her on one occasion seemingly threatening his mother for what must have been medication or drugs.

As the police had been in touch with the solicitors who owned the Mill, it was only a matter of putting in a request of intention for Florence to interview for the position of warden. However, it soon became clear that they did not think they needed to interview someone who had thwarted a potential drugs trafficking continuation. The fact that Florence was related to Liz was the added cherry on the cake and so it was that Florence would become the new warden starting immediately.

Florence being Florence, she decided that a good way to introduce herself at the Mill was with a party for the residents. She also decided that it couldn't wait, as if they waited until after the New Year some of them would have formed an opinion of her that would never be undone. So the party was to happen the day after tomorrow. Liz shrieked at her mother to give her a little more time.

"What on earth for, darling? We only need food, booze and a little music to make it go with a swing. I mean how much notice do you need? Easy peasy, darling, I used to do this at a moment's notice when I lived in Benidorm. And don't say it..."

"Ha, I wouldn't, Mum, it's so great to have you back. I'd almost forgotten how madcap you were at any given moment. Okay, we'll manage somehow. We'll raid my freezer and we have loads of the kinds of drink the elderly people enjoy such as sherry and port, et cetera – all the things that tend to get left at my own parties. As for the music, we don't want to overwhelm them; it's just as sort of background, isn't it? So, what about just Angus, me and Tom?"

"Yes, that's perfect, darling. Oh, don't let me forget to say thank you, darling, you are a little star to put up with me and not only that but find me a job and a place to live. It's going to be lovely, darling. I'll keep these old dears busy until they drop, and when they do eventually drop they'll have a smile on their lips."

"Oh, Mother! Ha ha, but I've no doubt they'll love you, Mum."

When Liz dropped her mother's idea on Tom she expected him to run for the hills at the thought of spending an afternoon with a load of old people just like his gran.

But he didn't. He was such a lovely lad – he went out of his way to make it the best afternoon ever. Liz had never seen him interact with such gusto. She saw Tom in the light of how his patients would see him in five or six years' time. He would be the young Dr Cassidy that at first no one wanted to see, because he was inexperienced, and then it would be, "I would like to see Dr Cassidy" because he was handsome and would remind them that they had once been young like him.

The afternoon was a great success and, as predicted, Florence won the hearts of not just the only two men residents, but also the women. She assured them that their proverbial feet would not touch the ground. She intended so many activities that they would need to clear their calendars. The look of those residents whose calendars had been empty for probably the last ten years other than for doctors', hospital or chiropodists' appointments was of pure excitement.

Angus, Isabel and Tom had worked their socks off. Liz had seen a side to Isabel she had never thought existed. She had a soft side that the elderly seemed to reach not only with Iona being Angus's mum but all of them. She had danced with the fitter of the residents, very carefully in case of too much excitement. She had sat among them and sung when the group had played Christmas carols. She had also waited on with food and gone from chair to chair for those who couldn't stand to go to the buffet table themselves. Isabel had shown hidden depths that only Liz had ever seen and now she knew it must be for the love of Angus, so to speak. He had brought out the maternal side of her.

The gig had been more exhausting than a night at the Duck but just as rewarding. To hear the residents asking Florence when she would be moving in, and saying that they couldn't wait was worth all of the rushing around, then the clearing up of it all. It had all been in a wonderful cause.

Chapter 36

Isabel rang Liz the following morning bright and early saying they should go into town to buy something to wear for Ben's New Year party.

"But I bought that lovely dress, I've only worn it the once. Do I have to go again?"

"Yes, you ninny. God, don't you know anything? He thought you looked gorgeous enough to eat in that, but now you need to put the cherry on the cake. Be ready in half an hour and I'll pick you up. I refuse to sit in that manky old van."

"Oh, all right, but I'm not tramping all over town just to tart myself up for Ben Paris, you know. I suppose if I bought a new dress it would come in for lots of occasions."

Liz prevaricated, but secretly thought it would be worth it to see that look again in Ben's eyes when he had seen her in her black dress. She hurried in and out of the shower and was standing at the door within the thirty minutes, even remembering to leave a note for Tom and her mother.

Isabel and Liz had known each other since they were children and had seen a lot of changes in relationships, mainly in Isabel, to be honest. However, Isabel hoped beyond hope that her best and kindest friend in the whole world would find happiness again. Maybe not like she had had with Bob, but as she herself felt happiness she had never thought she was ever likely to feel, she hoped for the same for her tiny warm-hearted friend.

After searching through lots of department stores and seeing nothing that jumped out at either Isabel or Liz, Isabel suddenly remember a little side street boutique that she said they simply had to try. Within minutes of entering the shop she had picked out a dress for Liz to try on and literally pushed her into the changing rooms, predicting that this would blow anyone's socks off who saw it.

"Oh my God, you look absolutely… Terrific. Turn around. Oh, my God, you've got a body to die for, you lucky devil. You must just love it to death, Liz, look at yourself."

Liz had looked at herself in the cubicle when she had poured herself into the sheer sheath of black stretch material. It was plain black crêpe, but that was the only thing that was plain about it. It literally was a sheath, which would show if a person had eaten a doughnut for breakfast.

Talk about a figure hugger, yet the neckline was so sweet – square, just nicely covering the cleavage, but promising so much more – and it had little cap sleeves. How could one describe it from the waist down? It clung so tightly and gave the body such a womanly shape that any man could be forgiven for looking much more than once.

"I am looking! God, Isabel, do I dare buy this? Do I not look like a, er, street walker?"

"Street walker? Since when do street walkers look like you? That dress on you has such va,va,voom, and you are the only person I know who could pull it off. And still be like Julie Andrews and Raquel Welch all at the same time, for goodness sake. You look beautiful but voluptuous, sexy yet subtle... Oh, for goodness sake, Liz, just buy the dress. If you never wear it again it will be worth every penny for Ben's New Year's Eve party. It'll knock his socks off, and seal his fate."

Convinced to buy the dress, though far from convinced that she would wear it for Ben's party, Liz turned her attention to Isabel's outfit. For a change Isabel had insisted on a trouser suit, a very slinky deep navy with silver sparkles. It had flowing trousers with wide legs and the top was a strapless basque but the finishing touch was a beautiful edge to edge jacket with the same silver sparkle woven through it. Isabel looked like Elizabeth Taylor, absolutely fabulous.

"You look like a real classy broad, Isabel, which is, I will lay money on, what my mother will say when she sees you in that. You look gorgeous, you must buy it. I must be mad, though, letting you persuade me into buying such a dress. You always do that, and I always let you. It's not me and I'll probably never wear it."

"I always persuade you and don't you always look terrific? Didn't he absolutely love you in the last one?"

"Yes."

"And didn't he love your little duffle jacket?"

"Yes."

"And don't you want to make an impression on him at the party?"

"Yes."

Isabel had trapped Liz into admitting she wanted Ben to notice her.

"Well, yes, I suppose so, but I don't want to cause a stir by looking half dressed, you know what I mean?"

"Don't be ridiculous, woman. Women reading the weather forecast wear dresses like that nowadays, and quite often they are pregnant… Ugh, no." Isabel pulled a face, imagining the dress with a bump in the middle.

"What I'm saying is that if you have the figure nowadays anything goes – it's cool to show off your figure. Whereas we kind of covered ours with tent-like garments when we were younger, now they put it all out there."

"Well, in that dress it will certainly all be out there, there's no denying that. And it does make me feel very sexy!"

"Well, there you are then, and what red-blooded male is not going to find you sexy in that dress?"

"I'm trying not to think what Tom, my mother or Bob would have made of it!"

"Liz, Bob loved the old you, the one that bought clothes from department stores and looked like everyone else and he loved you despite the horrendous clothes we often bought. But like any red-blooded male he would have whistled his head off if he had seen you in this dress. And he would not mind that you are beginning to feel like a woman again and are ready to move on; it doesn't mean you love him any less. So buckle up, girl, and get set for the party. And as for your mum and Tom, va, va, voom, they'll say."

Chapter 37

New Year's Eve dawned, crisp but clear. As no one except Liz was willing to sit in her van, which they said belonged to Barnie and it smelt like it, Isabel and Angus were to collect Florence and Tom. And Liz would follow in her own van. She was positive that there was a lot of diplomatic manoeuvring going on, giving Liz room to stay at Ben's if the need arose. Liz's guess would be that that would have been her mother's matchmaking idea. It was anything but subtle.

The party was in full swing as Liz pulled her little van into the packed drive of Juniper Manor. Every light in the house was on and she could hear the sound of music, although not the band – background music, for chatting, as she always thought of it at parties.

She parked the van, and as she climbed out she almost lost her nerve. She tugged the dress down to what she felt was a decent level above her knees. And she wrapped the beautiful Indian pashmina shawl firmly around her shoulders. She had bought it so that she didn't freeze to death, but mostly so that she didn't feel so exposed until she had mingled a little with the other guests. In the vain hope that there were one or two weather girls there in the same type of dresses.

No matter how slowly she walked up the drive, eventually she came to the door and had to go inside. As she entered the porch, which had been beautifully decorated in Christmas lights and which led into the large lobby, it would have been impossible to miss the gorgeous Christmas tree that Tom and Ben had put up between them. As she was admiring the Christmas tree, and not in any hurry to enter the throng of people, milling from room to room, she felt a warm breath on the bare skin at the back of her neck. The person whom she sensed was Ben. He drew in the deepest of breaths and almost a lung full of her perfume before turning her around to face him.

He unwound her from her pashmina and, if it were possible, took even more air into his already bursting lungs.

"Oh wow, you look, wow, and I mean that most sincerely… Wow! Are you the same person who was sat in my bath the first time we met?"

"Shush, you'll have the whole village thinking I've been in your bath."

Ben said in a stage whisper reply to her, "But you have! Sorry, I know I shouldn't tease you but you are so easy to tease, your cheeks go pink."

"I'm supposed to look sophisticated, not teasable and pink!"

"You look terrific and sophisticated, but I love to tease you anyway. I was panicking in case you weren't coming, but Tom and your mother assured me you were on your way."

"My mother, by the way, is Florence and she would love you to call her that. She feels younger when not being addressed as a mother. And I wouldn't dream of not coming to your party – you always come to mine, and this time I don't even have to cook or clean up… Do I?"

"No, you don't have to do anything except hold my hand and not move from my side all night, except when you play the fiddle, when you will be excused. But if Angus lifts you up tonight he better be careful what he grabs a hold of in that dress."

"Your Christmas tree is wonderful and really suits the large hallway just as I imagined when I decorated it."

Ben took hold of Liz's hand and pulled her towards the tree and indicated for her to take something off it. It was a small leather pouch tied with gold ribbon.

"Take the parcel off the tree and come with me; no one will miss us if they don't know you have arrived. They can't play any music without you, and they're all busy drinking and talking. Come, come."

Liz pulled the little bag off the tree and had no other choice but to follow him upstairs as he didn't let go of her hand for a second. As they reached the landing Liz knew where they were going and breathed a sigh of relief as this didn't seem the appropriate time to be visiting any of the bedrooms. It was quite clear that they were going into Ben's study. After they had entered the room Ben closed the door behind them firmly so as not to be disturbed. They sat down on the lovely sofa in the corner of his office and he eventually released her hand.

Liz looked at Ben properly for the first time other than a fleeting glimpse, and she saw that he had on a pristine white evening shirt with a cutaway collar opened at the neck, which allowed the deep cleft of his throat to be exposed. His dress trousers had a sheen of silk on the stripe, which went all the way down the sides, and you could see your face in the shine of his shoes. And he smelled delicious enough to eat.

“Please open your present, I have waited so long for you to come and pluck it off my tree. I thought I would go mad with the waiting for this night to come.”

Liz slowly opened the little leather bag. First of all she pulled out a piece of gold paper with some beautifully ciphered writing on it. But before she could read what it said, Ben told her to tip the bag up and find what was inside. Suddenly out slithered the most beautiful gold chain with a tiny gold…

“Ah, it’s a paintbrush, a tiny paintbrush. How absolutely gorgeous, thank you, Ben.”

“Now, now read the paper, please.”

Liz wasn’t sure what to expect. She thought it must be a night out somewhere special or a dinner date or a show even. But she certainly didn’t expect the words she read over and over twice before looking into Ben's face quizzically.

The note read:

> I hope by this time next year you will accept a smaller gold band???
>
> Merry Christmas Darling Lizy
>
> Love Ben
>
> Xxxx

Liz folded the note calmly, more calmly than she would ever have imagined, and looked at Ben's hopeful expression.

"Ben, can I ask you two questions before I give you my answer?"

"Yes, yes, anything. Whatever you need to know, ask."

"What is wrong with your heart? How bad is it?"

"How the…?"

"How isn't important at the moment. However, I'll tell you later how I know."

"Well, you know how I told you that I was a workaholic? Well, I was not only a workaholic, but I became obsessed with work. Building the business up, then when the business was doing well I wanted more and bigger contracts. Then I took on Fiona and I felt as though I should take more work on as there were two of us drawing salaries, so we needed more work. It became never-ending and I simply forgot about having a life. I ate and slept work. In fact, I often did just that. If I worked late I would literally sleep on the couch in my office until… One day I had what I thought was a heart attack."

Liz took a sharp intake of breath and held it, stopping herself from interrupting his story, but placing her hand on his in comfort.

"As it turns out, apparently, it was a combination of overwork, not enough exercise, bad eating habits, as in not eating at all, and the worst of all was I had been having irregular heart palpitations for months and had ignored them. Occasionally I would get a bit of a shock but I had never actually passed out with one until that day. I simply collapsed in the office and I knew nothing until I was in Edinburgh Royal Infirmary. I had extensive tests and the outcome was that I had an irregular heart beat, arrhythmia they call it. Which apparently one of our Prime Ministers has, and he carried on, doing his duty until his term was complete.

"So I have a temporary pacemaker. I have been assured that once my lifestyle has changed and my diet and general health improves then I will have no need for it. But it was enough to shock me into seeing the error of my ways, so to speak. I actually don't need to work as hard now. And I decide what work I choose to do. And the second question?"

"What is Fiona to you, apart from your business partner?"

“Fiona is, or rather was, my business partner and that is all! Oh, I know she gave the impression that we were more, but I can assure you that was more wishful thinking on her side. Why, I don’t know, I was no catch – work, work, work was all I ever cared about. In a way I think she was almost the same, but she felt it would be a more… solid, permanent arrangement if we were a couple. I don’t know. Maybe her biological clock was telling her it was almost too late. I’m not sure.

“However, you have no need to worry on that score, Fiona and I have officially separated the partnership. She wasn’t at all happy about it – she hoped that my buying this house and moving into the village was a whim and that I would go back to Edinburgh and life would carry on as usual. Once she realised I was serious, we agreed terms.

“She has bought me out, but we have made an agreement as I had fifty-one per cent of the company. It was my business in the first place, you see? We have agreed a figure, but also Fiona never wanted the larger, more challenging work that I loved yet often turned down in favour of the more lucrative bread and butter work. So we have agreed that any small work I hear about or am offered, I will give to her; and she will reciprocate by giving me the nod when a project comes up that she has no interest in, specialised work.

"When I was there last week to tie up some loose ends there was rather a handsome young, *very* young new architect in her office and she had moved up into mine. I got the impression that the young chap was so impressed with Fiona in more ways than one. He would be a much more willing companion, if you get my meaning.? Is that everything?"

"Well, almost." Liz squirmed a little but forced herself to ask the final question that, if not asked, would fester in her fertile mind.

"Why did Fiona stay at your house? Oh, I'm sorry, you don't have to answer that, I feel terrible now that I've even said it. I'm sorry, Ben, it's none of my business."

"You have every right to ask. I want everything between us to be open and honest. This house, as you know, has many bedrooms, and yes, she did stay over a couple of times, simply because it was too late for her to travel back to Edinburgh. But that was the only reason, I promise you. Also I gave her a key as it was Fiona who found me on the floor in my office and called the ambulance. So I suppose she thought she should carry on having a key until I returned to the fold, so to speak, and moved back to Edinburgh, and I never thought to ask for the key back once it became very obvious that Juniper Green is my home now."

"I feel terrible now for asking, it was none of my business… But I'm glad you told me, because I saw her car and it would have hurt me if you hadn't told me."

"Ah."

Liz told Ben how she had bumped into Fiona last week and had been told about his 'dicky' heart.

“I don’t think she meant it in a vicious way. But, to be honest, Liz, she must have felt as though, once I moved away from Edinburgh and started my new life in Juniper Green, it was obvious I was happier than she had ever seen me. I was enjoying life, meeting people. I had met you and your wonderful family and friends. It must have seemed obvious to her that my attraction to you was almost instant and overwhelming. And the life we had shared in Edinburgh was slipping away. I think she has only just realised since taking on her new apprentice that life could be as good for her as it is for me, now that she has relinquished any idea of us becoming a couple. Now can I say one thing before you give me your answer?”

Liz nodded.

“No one could fail to see how much in love you were with your husband, and I respect that, and will never, ever attempt to replace him in anyway. Not that anyone ever could. I will only say this – that from what I’ve heard about Bob from you and all of his friends and family, especially Tom, he would never have wanted you to end up alone. You have so much love to give, you are the kindest most contented woman I have ever met, and I would like to add to that, not take from it. I would like you to consider… that we, er, court? Is that still an expression? Well, you know what I mean, be a couple and whenever you feel the time is right, I would like you to marry me!"

"Oh, Ben, you are a really wonderful person yourself, and how on earth you weren't snapped up long before now, despite your burying yourself in your work, I'll never know."

Ben looked at that moment terrified that there was going to be a 'but'…

"And when 'we' think the time is right, then I would like nothing better than to marry you!"

Ben suddenly jumped up, taking Liz with him into his arms, and twirled around and around the room until they came to rest.

When Ben sat on the edge of his desk with Liz perched almost on top of him, she suddenly noticed a large silver photo frame.

"What the…? Is that me? When did you…?"

"I took it that day at the castle and I knew the instant I saw it on my camera that I would frame it and keep it forever on my desk, so that I could look at it every day. Even if we were never destined to be more than friends I would always have that day."

Liz looked into Ben's eyes and his heart melted, as his head descended and his lips fixed upon her half-open and willing mouth. They kissed and Ben's hands began to stray over Liz's body in her stretch crêpe dress, which left nothing to the imagination.

Then he placed Liz gently down, saying at the same time as he sucked in a lung full of air, "We had better go down and meet and greet as I don't think it's a good idea for me to be alone with you in that dress."

"Oh, you don't like my dress? I've been told that even weather girls wear them on television nowadays," Liz said with a coquettish downward flick of her eyelashes, and a knowing smile, as to the effect the dress was having on him.

"I don't suppose I would notice if a parade of girls wore dresses like that, but with you inside it, it is irresistible. It has the effect of me needing to touch you so I think for the sake of my equilibrium we had better go down and join our guests. But first…"

He retrieved the gold necklace with the tiny gold paintbrush attached and placed it around Liz's neck. As he did so he leant down and kissed the nape of her neck. Then his hands began their wayward roam of her curves once again.

"No, no, let's go," said Liz. "The sooner we go, the sooner we can come back."

As they walked down the stairs, hand in hand, Liz said it had only just dawned on her that Tom must have seen the photo of her on the study desk when he had shown him round the house and that must have been why his conversation had seemed to have withheld something.

"He's a nice guy, Tom," said Ben. "You and Bob did a good job – he'll make a fine doctor, because he cares about people. It goes without saying about his need to protect you! But I have assured him that I would never hurt you or let anything hurt you as long as I live. And, you know, he said he believed me, which I thought was nice."

"So he knew you were planning some sort of surprise tonight? Is that why no one would come in my van? They are probably going to make a discreet exit giving me 'space', as they say. How embarrassing."

"Not really – they only want nice things for you, because they all love you, as I do. And you are a grown woman and they know grown-up people… sleep together… eventually, but there is no pressure. Not from me, I can assure you, so at the end of the night, if you want me to take you home, then that's what will happen without any regrets… Well, maybe just a few."

As he said it he kissed her nose, just before they entered the throng of happy party people.

When they arrived downstairs and entered the large sitting room packed with party folk, like bees to a honey pot Isabel and Florence dashed across to Liz. And within seconds of arriving, an almighty squeal went up and Liz was being hugged to within an inch of her life. Liz looked across at Ben, whose back was being slapped heartily by Angus and Tom, and they gave each other a brief understanding but rueful smile.

Then above their immediate eye contact and bliss a chant could be heard:

"Rovers, Rovers, Rovers."

It was at that point that someone handed Liz her fiddle and, having no other option, she was about to play when Angus went to lift her up so she could not only be seen but also heard among the din of the crowd. Out of nowhere a large pair of hands took hold of Liz's tiny waist and Ben gave Angus a possessive smile from ear to ear, to which Angus gave a mock bow. Ben lifted Liz on to the solid tiled coffee table, and as she stood in her stockinged feet on the table in 'that dress' her figure almost mirrored that of her fiddle… fantastic!

This time, the first song they played was 'The Wild Rover' to shouts of delight. The night was one of the best nights anyone could remember, the music and the atmosphere were fabulous, and in between Ben and Liz stayed close to each other and even the touch of his fingers lightly on hers was electrifying, sending shivers through her whole body. She knew without a doubt, too, that the same feelings were running through Ben.

Midnight arrived and the whole room counted down. It was fairly obvious where Isabel, Angus, Liz and Ben would be, which was as close to each other as they could be in order that they could take full advantage of the first and last chime of the clock. Ben and Liz went into the lobby and stood in the darkness save for the lights of the Christmas tree, as the clock struck midnight. Ben wrapped his arms around Liz and she stood on the bottom step so that she could totally reciprocate his hold. This was truly a kiss they would remember forever, no matter what happened after this night, and to think… It could only get better from now until next year at this time.

Everyone began to leave, and the house emptied. The caterers had been clearing and packing as the evening had gone on, leaving Ben's home almost as magically tidy as if there hadn't been a party. Liz said reluctantly that it was time for her to go, too.

Tom had left with a young girl from the village – he'd left his car in Ben's drive and walked off into the night with the young lady. Florence, Angus and Isabel had also decided to walk, so their car was also left abandoned in Ben's drive. Liz wrapped herself into her pashmina and began her walk to the front door with Ben at her side. As they arrived at the door and began the long goodnight kiss, it became quite obvious that Liz was going nowhere this night. Ben looked into her eyes for approval, which he saw without waiting for the answer. He carried her up the stairs almost without breaking their kisses.

They entered Ben's bedroom, which Liz had only ever glanced inside, since the time when she had had on her working dungarees. Never in a million years had she ever thought she would be the one to sleep in this sumptuous bed with the most gorgeous owner of Juniper Manor.

As they were wrapped together like writhing snakes they fell softly to the fluffy quilt and Ben ran his hands almost frantically over Liz's curves, her hips, her womanly breasts, which seemed to grow with every touch. Ben's breath came in pants and gasps, as did Liz's. He slowly began to peel away her seductive dress and the only sound that could be heard, apart from their joint gasps for air, was Ben telling her never to part with that dress!

There was no more coherent talk, simply groans of pleasure and the sound of passionate exchanges. The next words uttered were Ben saying to his beloved Liz, “Happy New Year, darling.”

And Liz’s reply was, “And to you, my darling, until next year, sweet Benjamin!”

Epilogue

The year that followed was a fresh start for more than Liz and Ben; it was like fresh footprints in the pure driven snow for our entire little group. For Florence, it was what she had been looking for and needed. She found she really was a born organiser, for once she had moved into the Mill, from day one, her first decree was that those who lived within had a choice, but she requested that, just like in a university dormitory, they propped their front doors open.

"To heck," she said with the fire regulations. The dividing fire doors were so heavy that a person was in danger of being stuck between the doors even if there wasn't a fire. She explained to all the residents at their first meeting that at universities students arrived alone, scared and without their usual network of friends. So it was a great way of making new networks. But here in the Mill they had a head start, because they had all grown up knowing of each other's existence, even if they hadn't been bosom pals. However, once their front door was closed they were in danger of being lonely in a building full of potential friends.

She then went from strength to strength, organising tea dances at least once a week, inviting members of the public to join in; whist clubs who could meet as many times as they wished; bingo with prizes rather than money, for those who didn't have the ability to go shopping for the odd little present. She had devised a stand up and sit down bingo for those who were more disabled than others.

She organised with Liz that the group would play for special events. She also opened the kitchen to those who wanted to help and even do a little baking, under her supervision, of course. She invited members from other villages to join in any of their projects, such as making shoeboxes for good causes. All of the projects she organised could be attended by those who were more disabled, but could still help with and feel a part of any good cause.

As for Angus and Isabel, it wasn't long before they wanted to spend every day together, so that's just what they did. However, they decided that the magic piece of paper that Isabel had set such store by had only brought her bad luck in the past so this time around she and Angus would live together in her cottage, as Angus lived in a furnished flat on the outskirts of the village. Isabel's cottage was far too large for her by herself anyway, but she loved it so much and wouldn't ever sell it, so it was decided and they were blissfully happy.

They were very happy and comfortable with each other, so when Isabel suggested to Angus that his mother would be very welcome to move into the granny flat attached to the cottage, they asked her that day.

"It's very kind of you both, and I thank you for the offer. Had Mrs Monroe still been the warden, I may have taken you up on it.

But… Since Florence has taken over… Well, how can I put it? You must be joking! It's the best place in the world, there is so much going on, and I have met so many people and I haven't enjoyed myself so much in years."

Tom had gone back to university with a part of his heart missing. He had unexpectedly and out of the blue fallen head over heels for the young lady he had taken home on the night of the New Year's Eve party at Ben's last year.

Ben and Liz were even more blissfully happy than any two people could expect to be. Liz spent as much time at Ben's as she did at home. Therefore they had bought a new bed for Barnie who was equally at home in front of the Rayburn, as he was by Liz's Aga. And as for the midnight thinking sessions on the common, they hadn't stopped either. In fact, they had become a ritual, when they were working on a joint project, which they did almost all the time now. Instead of Ben struggling with it on his own, he now had Liz to back him, to comfort him, and to put in a full stop and say it was time to let it go until another day.

She was able to persuade him in a way that only she had the power to do, which usually always ended up in their large comfortable bed. It was after a very satisfying conclusion had been achieved and they were still wrapped in each other's arms that Liz said, "Yes."

"Yes what, my darling?"

"Yes, I will marry you. In fact, I can't wait and would like to be married before Christmas so that on New Year's Eve, standing under our tree in the lobby, we will be Mr and Mrs Paris."

Ben rolled Liz on top of him and looked into her face as he often did, but this time it was different. He had a look of complete wonderment and happiness on his face as he kissed her thoroughly and agreed that it would be done.

They were married on Christmas Eve, in the village church, with the whole village, it seemed, in attendance. Liz and Isabel had, of course, had a shopping spree for Liz's outfit; however, there was no skimpy crêpe dress. She wore a much more demure cream suit in a military style, the cropped jacket and pencil straight skirt suiting her figure to perfection. In contrast, Ben looked tall, dark and handsome in his charcoal Joseph Turner suit, his pristine white shirt and tasteful red tie and matching cufflinks.

Florence was beside herself with excitement – her mission, she felt, was complete. Her daughter was married again. Of course, it wasn't a white wedding, because Bob was and always would be Liz's first love.

But Florence knew that this marriage was made to last and would be enduring and happy, as both Ben and Liz loved each other deeply. For Liz and Ben, life would become a coalition of talents and challenges that each of them would find stimulating, but most of all enjoyable. Liz was determined that Ben would enjoy his work again without the pressure that had almost destroyed him.

They had a small reception at Juniper Manor, where they spent their first night of marriage. However, Ben had a surprise for Liz. He knew her overriding wish was to stand under their own Christmas tree at midnight on New Year's Eve. But as a present for completing the Muir of Ochil Castle, the owners had suggested, as they would be away in Austria skiing, that Ben and his new wife spend a few days there for their honeymoon. Then he would whisk her back for their new tradition of a New Year's Eve party to bring in the New Year for all of their friends and family – which is exactly what they did. And who's to say that on the following year, as they stood under their Christmas tree, there wouldn't be an addition to their own family.

The End

www.ingramcontent.com/pod-product-compliance
Lightning Source LLC
Chambersburg PA
CBHW030821310726
48980CB00006B/584/J

* 9 7 8 0 9 5 6 5 8 5 0 7 3 *